The Devil Wears Timbs VI

The Devil Wears Timbs 6

Copyright © 2018 Tranay Adams. All rights reserved.

Warning: The unauthorized reproduction or distribution of this work is illegal. Criminal copyright infringement, including infringement without monetary gain, is investigated by FBI and is punishable by up to five (5) years in federal prison and a fine of $250,000.

All names, characters, and incidents depicted in this book are products of the author's imagination or are used fictitiously. Any resemblance to actual events, locales, organizations, or persons, living or dead, is entirely coincidental, and beyond the intent of the author and publisher.

No part of this book may be reproduced or transmitted in any form or by any means, electronic or mechanical, including photocopying, recording, or by any information storage and retrieval system, without permission in writing from the publisher.

The Devil Wears Timbs 6/ Tranay Adams-1st ed. © 2018

ISBN: 978-1-7377789-3-6

Email: dopereadzpresents@gmail.com

Facebook: Tranay Adams

Instagram: Tranay Adams

Cover Artist: J Ash Brown

The Devil Wears Timbs VI
Just Like Daddy
By Tranay Adams

PROLOGUE

Year 2039

The sky was the prettiest midnight blue. The moon was full and shining brightly. The suburb was quiet, but this wasn't unusual for a neighborhood where the wealthy held residence. The noisy crickets in the grass were the only reoccurring sound besides the humming of a very large engine, which was ripping up the residential street at the moment. The enormous truck was going so fast debris and lose trash was flying up in the air.

The vehicle flying up the street was a black on black Ford F-150 pickup truck. It was complete with four large lights that resided on its rooftop. Mounted over its grill was a front end that belonged on a bulldozer called a Blade. The pickup was sitting up high on shiny rims and thirty-six inch tires. The tires made the vehicle look like it was a monster truck.

The occupants of the Ford were two hulking men. One was behind the wheel while the other sat in the driver seat. The one in the driver seat head moved from left to right, looking at the addresses of the homes they drove passed.

He looked down at the address written on the piece of spiral notebook paper. Once he was sure the address was cemented in his mind, he balled up the paper and threw it out of the window. He then pulled on his black leather gloves and flexed his fingers in them.

Afterwards, he continued to look for the address of the estate he had in mind. Seeing the location to the left of him, he nudged homeboy behind the wheel and pointed to the mansion sitting far away from the gates. The driver gave him a nod and floored the gas pedal. The red needle on the speedometer sped around in a circle, climbing in speed. The F-150 became a flash in darkness it was going so fast in the night. The gates of the mansion appeared to becoming larger and larger the closer the pickup truck came into contact with them. The huge vehicle had gotten about ten feet away from the gates, before the surveillance cameras residing on either side of them zeroed in on the Ford pickup.

Ba-boom!

The gates swung inward as the F-150 collided with them. As soon as the truck crossed the threshold an alarm sounded off, blaring loudly. The large florescent flood lights surrounding the mansion popped on and overwhelmed the occupants of the truck with their illumination. It appeared as if the illumination coming from the flood lights were going to zap the men into dust it was so bright. The men occupying the Ford were unbothered though. They slipped on high tech goggles that allowed them to see through the rays of the lights.

The dude on the passenger side let his window complete down and climbed out of it. He got upon the rooftop and hunched down, holding onto the black bars that held the truck's flood lights in place. His eyes locked on the double doors of the estate. That's where he was headed as soon as the transporting vehicle stopped.

"Leave now, you're trespassing on private property, and if you proceed any further, you will be punished to the full extent of the owner." A feminine British voice rang out of the loudspeakers hidden somewhere on the estate. When the other surveillance cameras on the grounds lenses pushed outward and zeroed in on the F-150, which was still flying towards the mansion, the voice continued, "Very, well then, you have been warned."

Instantly, 50 caliber machineguns came up from the rose bushes in front of the mansion and focused in on the speeding pickup truck. As soon as the Ford stopped, the machineguns rattled to life spitting hot flames. The bullets spitting out of the hollowed barrels of the weapons looked more like lasers than ammunition.

Ping! Ting! Zing! Bing! Ring! Kiiiing! Chiiiiiing!

The bullets deflected off of the windshield, blade and hood of the Ford pickup truck. The vehicle was enforced by bulletproof material that was durable enough to stop a fucking grenade round. The machineguns finished spitting and their barrels wafted with smoke. The empty shell casings from their firing lie around them on the ground.

Seeing that the machineguns had finished firing, homeboy on the rooftop ran down the hood of the Ford and did a summer salt off of it. He landed in a kneeling position with his hands flat on the ground. Hearing the barking of angry dogs in the darkness on either side of him, his ears slightly jumped. This prompted him to look from left to right. In slow motion, he saw pit bulls coming at him full speed ahead. The beasts sped up to him and he rose to his feet, prepared to brawl with them.

Brack! Wap! Wamm!

Old boy punched the pit bulls out of the air that leaped up at him. He kicked the third one down and it crashed to the ground, hard. He moved his head back as a fourth hound went flying across his line of vision. Homeboy grabbed the dog by one of his hind legs. Using all of his might, he slammed the beast on either side of him, repeatedly. Once he figured that the hound was out of the fight, he held it up and looked at it closely. Its eyes were rolled to their whites and its tongue was hanging out of its mouth, lifelessly. It was dead!

The intruder dropped the dead dog at his feet. When the remaining pit bulls flew up at him, he extended a twenty inch blade from his sleeve and chopped one of their heads off. He then stabbed another one through its heart and grabbed the last one by its neck. The pit bull tried to bite him in his face. Slowly, the man squeezed the dog's throat causing it to squirm, uncomfortably. The beast gasped and whimpered. Finally, the intruder ended the animal's suffering. He grabbed the pit bull by its skull and tore it from between its shoulders. Its bloody spinal cord dripped on the lawn. Tossing both halves of the pit bull on the surface, the intruder drew his blade back into his sleeve and went charging up the steps of the mansion.

****

Ba-doom! Ba-doom! Boom!

The entire mansion seemed to shake as its entrance doors were assaulted with brute force. The doors rattled and rattled until they swung inward. The dude that rode in on the rooftop of the F-150 truck walked in over the threshold. His head was on a swivel. His terrifying eyes peered out of the holes of the mask. Once he located the staircase, he went running towards it. He'd just placed his boot on the first step when he was met by the round of a high caliber handgun. The impact of the slug slammed into him, causing him to stumble backwards, bumping into the wall. He looked up to see Kingston hurrying down the steps towards him. Outstretched before him was a black handgun with an infrared laser, which he gripped with both hands.

"You broke into the wrong mansion, asshole!" A mad dogging Kingston reported. He was shirtless and wearing pajama pants.

The intruder scowled from behind his mask. He and Kingston went charging after one another. Kingston stopped halfway down the staircase and trained his infrared laser on the intruder's heart, squeezing rapidly. The gun slightly bucked as spat fire from its barrel.

Choot! Choot! Choot! Choot!

Each bullet that struck the intruder sent him propelling backwards, until he finally fell to the floor. He lay there still as Kingston cautiously approached him, gun trained on his forehead. If he so much as blinked then the next bullet was going straight through his forehead.

"Kingston, are you, okay?" Eureka called out from the top of the staircase. She was standing beside Tristan. They both had handguns and were in their pajamas.

"I'm good, ma. I got his ass!" Kingston claimed as he cautiously moved in closer to his victim. Once he was standing over him, he kept his gun trained on his forehead as he leaned in to pull the mask off his head. Suddenly, the intruder's eyelids snapped open and he smacked the gun from out of his face. The shot went wild and the handgun went sliding across the floor, spinning in circles. It didn't stop until it bumped against the wall.

The intruder kicked Kingston in his torso and sent him slamming against the wall. He then jumped upon his booted feet and thrashed his arms. This movement caused twenty inch blades to extend out of the sleeves of his thermal. The soft light kissed off the blades and gleams swept up the lengths of them.

"Shoot 'em!" Tristan called out as he pointed his handgun at the intruder. Eureka was right behind him pointing her handgun at his ass, too.

"Nah, be easy, I got 'em." Kingston composed himself and slid into a martial arts fighting stance. He then tucked his chin and raised his fists, before his eyes. Ready to brawl now, he motioned the intruder to engage him with the wave of his hand. "Bring that ass here!"

The intruder engaged Kingston swinging his deadly blades at his head and feet. The young man moved with the speed and agility of a cat, dodging the blades easily. He countered by firing punches in every exposed part of his opponent's body, but the blows he landed didn't do anything to slow the man down. On top of that, he felt like he was slamming his fists into a brick wall. Before Kingston knew it, his face and body was shiny from perspiration. He was breathing heavily and exhausted. He threw all of his best moves at the intruder and it didn't do anything to faze him.

The intruder, seeing that Kingston had grown exhausted, drew his blades back inside of his sleeves. He then launched his attack, throwing punches, backhands and kicks into every exposed part of his body. The last blow he landed against Kingston dropped the youngsta down to his hands and knees. He rasped out of breath having had the wind knocked out of him. Seeing that he wasn't in any shape to carry on the fight, the intruder pulled him back up by the back of his neck. He extended the blade out of his right sleeve and moved to stab him through his face with it. The blade twinkled at its tip, but before he could deliver the kill-shot, gunfire erupted. The reoccurring gunfire made it sound like firecrackers popping inside of the mansion.

The first wave of bullets slammed into the intruder, but then he extended his second blade from his left sleeve. He swiftly moved his blades and deflected the bullets as they came at him, making sparks fly everywhere. Once the firing had ceased, the last of the bullets fell at his boots. When he looked up, he saw Eureka and Tristan ejecting the magazines from out of the bottoms of their handguns. Seeing this, he pulled out his own handgun. He dove to the floor, tucking and rolling. He came back up on his bending knee, gripping his handgun with both hands. He angled his head to the side and pointed the lethal end of his handgun at Eureka. Acknowledging that Eureka hadn't finished loading her gun yet, Tristan dove in front of her and took the bullet that was meant to take her life. He howled in pain and fell to the steps, dropping his gun. Eureka's eyes lit up with concern. Fearing the worse, she looked down at Tristan and checked his wound. Seeing that it wasn't life threatening, she returned to the firefight.

"You bastard!" Eureka angled her head and pointed her handgun at the intruder, squeezing the trigger with succession. One bullet struck the intruder in the chest and the next one took the gun out of his hand. Seeing that he was on the losing end of the battle, the intruder snatched Kingston up and held the blade to his throat. The tip of the blade pierced the soft flesh of his neck and caused blood to trickle.

"Wait, no, stop!" Eureka panicked and lowered her handgun.

"Drop the gun! Drop it now, goddamn it or I swear I'll slit his shit right now!" the intruder swore as he slowly came up the steps.

"Alright, okay." Eureka said, dropping her gun and lifting her hands in the air in surrender.

"Now, lay on your stomach, and I swear on my life if you try anything, I'll cut his fuckin' head off…don't try me, bitch! Got it?"

"Yes, I got it. I won't try anything, just don't hurt my son." Eureka did as she was told, lying on her stomach on the staircase.

The intruder dragged Kingston up the steps until he reached his parents. Once he did, he dropped him at his feet and pointed his wrist at him. A small metal barrel emerged from his sleeve and he pressed the center of his black leather glove with his middle fingers. When he did this, it triggered a hidden mechanism. Instantly, a green gas sprayed out of the small metal barrel, knocking Kingston out cold. The intruder then turned to Eureka and Tristan, spraying them with the gas and knocking them out as well.

Having seen that Eureka and Tristan were asleep, the intruder made his way up the staircase stealthily. He placed his back up against the wall once he reached the landing, inching his way towards Tristan and Eureka's daughter, Cyan's bedroom door. Hunching down, he made his way towards the door and kneeled down to the lock. Fishing his tongue around inside of his mouth, he pushed two bobby pins out from between his lips. He plucked the bobby pins out of his mouth and jimmied the lock until it opened. Once the door popped open, he pocketed the bobby pins and stood up. He grasped the doorknob and gently pushed his way inside of Cyan's bedroom. He got the door halfway open when he looked up to see her standing before him. She was a beautiful Mahogany complexioned girl with her hair styled in box braids, which had purple streaks in them.

Cyan eyebrows slanted and her nose scrunched up. She locked her teeth and her jaws pulsated. She held a shotgun at her side that looked like it was bigger than her. For a minute she and the intruder stood there staring at one another. Within the blink of an eye, she was pulling the trigger of her 12 gauge shotgun. The powerful weapon roared at her side unleashing a cloud of smoke and sparks. The impact from the shotgun's blast sent the intruder slamming up against the door and falling flat on his stomach. He lay where he was motionless, breathless.

A fearless Cyan slowly approached her victim with her shotgun trained on him. She took precautions in her approach. For all she knew the mothafucka that broke into the mansion was playing possum. She got about three feet away from the intruder when she narrowed her eyelids and angled her head.

"Mothafucka, you ain't dead!" Cyan declared. She then blasted on his ass three more times. As soon as she ceased fire smoke wafted from the barrel of her shotgun. Things were quiet and still for a while, and then the intruder's blade extended out of his right sleeve. Seeing this, Cyan's eyes doubled in size and she went to fire on him again. Her reaction time was a little too slow, because he'd already swiped his blade across the shotgun, cutting it completely in half and making it useless.

Cyan looked to the halves of the shotgun on the floor in disbelief. Before she knew it, the intruder was springing to his feet with the agility of a ninja. Snapping herself out of her daze, Cyan threw up her fists and got into a fighting stance. She went at homeboy with all she had. Many of her attacks connected but they didn't do anything to faze the man. Although she was quicker and far more skilled in hand to hand combat than her opponent, her attacking him was a waste of time. He was far more powerful than her and had a high tolerance for pain.

The intruder gave Cyan a flurry of punches to her mid section and cracked her in the jaw, twice. He followed up by punching her square in the face. She went to fall to the carpet but he grabbed her by the collar of her gown, stopping her in mid-fall. He then sprayed her in the face with his sleeping gas which put her out for the count. Afterwards, he hoisted her over his shoulder and brought his right wrist to his mouth. He spoke to his partner through a radio transceiver.

"Bring the truck around to the east end of the mansion. I'm in the third bedroom on the right side…second floor. You can't miss me." Once the intruder had run down the information to his partner-in-crime, he picked up the shotgun that was once in Cyan's possession. He lifted the shotgun and aimed it at the window of the young girl's bedroom.

"Cyan? Cyan? I'm coming, baby, momma's coming." Eureka called out weakly.

The intruder looked over his shoulder hearing Eureka's voice coming from outside of the door. From the noise she was making he could tell she was coming up the steps as fast as she could. That didn't leave much time to react, so he had to be fast with his next action. The intruder pointed his shotgun at corners of the window and pulled the trigger. The powerful weapon jerked in his gloved hand and shattered the glass. The broken glass went flying out of the window and the wind sucked the curtains outward, leaving them ruffling on the outside of the window. A cool breeze rushed into the bedroom, but the intruder could only feel a hint of it.

Hearing his partner contacting him, the intruder threw the empty shotgun down to the floor. He then pressed his finger against the ear-bud in his ear and listened to what he was being told. He then brought his wrist back to his mouth and told him that he was on his way.

"Stop!" Eureka appeared in the door of the bedroom. She looked sluggish, but the will of a mother was powerful. "Put her down, you son of a bitch!"

An angered Eureka came charging inside of the bedroom after the intruder. Still holding Cyan over his shoulder, he whipped around as she reached him. She came at him with everything she had and he deflected it all with one hand. Seeing that she wasn't landing any blows, Eureka went that much harder at homeboy. She landed three solid blows to his face and then she leaped up, bringing the heel of her foot across his jaw. The force behind the attack sent the intruder flying to the side dropping Cyan to the carpet.

Eureka landed on her feet and got right back into a fighting stance. She breathed heavily as she mad dogged the floored home invader. Her fists were up and ready and so were her feet.

Come on! Stay down, stay down, you son of a bitch, Eureka thought to herself seeing her opponent lying on his back. Suddenly, the fingers of his right hand twitched and she said 'fuck' under her breath. This was because she'd already launched an attack against him with everything she had to give. If it wasn't for the gas weakening her, Eureka was sure she would have been able to take the dude.

Boom!

Anton kicked the door open as he entered Cyan's bedroom. He was in a wife beater and boxer briefs. He clutched his black handgun at his waist. His eyes moved around the bedroom until they landed on the home invader. As soon as he spotted him, homeboy's back rose from the floor and he pointed his right fist at Eureka. Seeing something long and metal gleaming, Anton peered closely and saw that it was a twenty inch blade in homeboy's sleeve. His head whipped back and forth between Eureka and the blade. Anton went to open fire on the home invader, but he'd already fired the blade at his sister. Seeing the blade en route to his sister, Anton called out to her. His calls fell on deaf ears because she was like a deer caught in headlights seeing the blade zeroing in on her.

"Get...down!" Anton called out to Eureka as he ran towards her. His voice sounded demonic and everything appeared to be moving in slow motion. "Uuhhh!" He flew through the air and knocked her out of the way, putting himself in the way of danger. The sharp projectile glinted as it soared through the air. It pierced Anton's shoulder and lodged its self halfway through it, sending him flying backwards. The blade embedded him to the wall where he screamed at the top of his lungs in agony, still holding his handgun at his side.

Eureka ran over to Anton trying to figure out how to get him off the wall and off the blade.

"No, take the gun, save Cyan." Anton winced as he urged his sister and nodded to the intruder. When Eureka looked over her shoulder, she found dude scooping her daughter into his arms. Quickly, she snatched the handgun from her brother and whipped around. She was just in time to see the back of the intruder. He was cradling Cyan in his arms and was squatting down on the window pane, attempting to leap out of the window. Eureka squeezed her left eyelid shut and angled her head as she took aim with her gun. She squeezed the trigger of her handgun with succession. The weapon jumped slightly as it spat fire. The intruder took three bullets to the back like it wasn't anything. He then leaped off the window pane. Seeing him disappear through the shattered window, Eureka ran over to the widow and looked down. At that moment, see saw a pickup truck speeding towards the gates entrance. Her daughter and the intruder were in the flatbed of the truck. The intruder laid Cyan down in the bed and looked up at Eureka. He smiled up at her and kissed the palm of his hand, blowing her a kiss.

"Noooooo, noooooo, noooooooo!" Eureka screamed and screamed as tears cascaded down her cheeks.

THE DEVIL WEARS TIMBS VI

CHAPTER ONE

Two years later/Rio De Janeiro

Blatatatatatatatat!

AK-47s shook as they spat flames at the back of a fleeing man in a duster, making the ground explode in chunks of dirt and debris around him. The man fled up the street, but every now and again he'd spare a glance over his shoulder to see how far behind the gunmen were that were after him.

"Haa! Haa! Haa! Haa!" the fleeing man huffed and puffed as he ran. He was moving like a track star up the block, making the surrounding huts look like blurs.

The floodlights and headlights of the raggedy Toyota pickup truck that was carrying the gunmen shined on the fleeing man's back. One of the men that were standing up in the flatbed looked thirtyish.

He was wearing a dull red backwards baseball cap and a gray bandana over the lower half of his face that looked like it had been around for ages. Determination was in his eyes as he ejected the banana clip from out of his AK-47 and smacked in a new one. While he was doing this, his homeboy that was back there with him was trying to un-jam his AK-47. He was wearing a neoprene mask over the lower half of his face and a chain of copper jacketed bullets over his shoulder. Once he'd finished un-jamming his assault rifle, he stood up and started spitting fire at Goldie again. As he was busting at Goldie, homie wearing the baseball cap was locking a jacketed bullet into his choppa.

Blatatatatatatatatat! Buratatatatat!

"Haa! Haa! Haa! Haa! Haa!" Goldie huffed and puffed as he hauled ass. His face was shiny from sweat and his long blonde dread locks were bouncing, tapping against the shoulders of his duster. More Chunks of the ground and debris flew up into the air as the bullets from the AKs struck the surface at his heels. He hoisted up the two M-16's to his shoulders. The nigga was exhausted and he wasn't sure how long he could keep running.

Blatatatatatatatatat

The fool wearing the neoprene mask brows furrowed seeing that his choppa jammed on him again.

"Fuck! The bitch done jammed up on me again!" he spat angrily and tried to fix his assault rifle. Homie wearing the baseball cap glanced at him but kept firing at Goldie.

"Fuck it, dawg! It's do or die!" Goldie said to no one in particular. He then said it louder, "Do or die, mothafuckaz!"

Goldie dove to the left, tucking and rolling. He came back up on one knee, holding up his M-16's and pointing them at the nigga that was shooting at him. Homie in the baseball cap was bringing his AK around when he was suddenly pelted with ammunition. He did a little dance on his feet and fell out of the side of the pickup truck. Once he was dispatched, Goldie set his sights on dude wearing the neoprene mask. One of his M-16's clicked empty so he tossed it aside and gripped his last one with both hands. He squeezed the trigger of his weapon and it rattled to life spitting fire and blowing his target's skull apart. Goldie's victim fell over inside of the flatbed of the pickup, but the Toyota kept coming at him. The headlights of the vehicle blinded him. The next thing he knew it was slamming into him and he was going over the hood of it. Goldie rolled upon the windshield of the pickup and tumbled down to the street.

"Ughhh!" Goldie winced. Looking up, he saw a shadowy figure hop out of the passenger seat of the Toyota with what he believed was a handgun. Seeing that his life was in danger, he took off running as fast as he could. He didn't have time to search for his M-16. Homeboy with the gun was on him like stink on shit!

"Haa! Haa! Haa! Haa! Haa!" Goldie glanced over his shoulder as he ran. He pulled out a machete from where he had it sheathed inside of the recess of his duster. His eyes were locked on kids' sword fighting with sticks in the middle of street. When he spotted the youngest and smallest of the bunch an idea came to mind. Running through the middle of the children, he snatched up the boy he'd set his sights on and ran upon the curb. The youngsta cried out in distress, but the kids he'd been playing with looked helpless. They watched as Goldie fled up stone steps.

Just then, the dude with the gun ran through the crowd of children and went after Goldie. He ran up the steps past huts made out of old scrap material and structures without windows and rooftops. Sheathing his machete, Goldie held the boy against his chest and jumped up. He grabbed the edge of a hut's roof and pulled himself upon it. The nigga that was on his ass was right behind him, tucking his gun and climbing the roof after him.

Still holding the boy he'd snatched up in the street, Goldie fled towards the end of the rooftop. He lost his balance and nearly fell, but then he quickly righted himself. He continued on until he reached the edge of the rooftop. Looking down, he saw that the ground was much further below. If he were to jump he was positive he'd break both of his legs, so he'd have to think of another way to get away from dude pursuing him. Looking at the rooftop across from him, Goldie noticed that it was entirely too far for him to leap upon so he'd have no choice but to face his enemy.

"Fuck, fuck, fuck! Think, think, think," Goldie squeezed his eyelids shut and punched himself in the forehead. "Okay, fuck it!" he snatched his machete free from where he'd placed it and turned around. He sat the boy down in front of him and placed the machete against his throat. The youngsta's eyes bulged and he clenched his jaws. He stood on the tips of his sneakers feeling the machete against his neck and held on to Goldie's arm, fearful of having his throat sliced.

"Back up! Back the fuck up, or I'll slit this lil' mothafucka'z throat from ear to ear! I swear on my brotha's grave, I will."

Goldie mad dogged the man who was slowly walking in his direction. The mothafucka didn't heed his warning so he had to let him know he was dead ass serious. "Oh, you wanna test my gangsta, bitch?" The man continued in his direction, until he saw him press the machete against the boy's neck, drawing a trickle of blood. Seeing the child whimper made the man stop in his tracks.

"Zachary! Zachary!" a woman called out below.

"Momma, momma, momma!" the boy in Goldie's clutches called out to his mother with tears sliding down his cheeks.

"Oh, God, please, don't hurt him! Don't hurt my baby!" the woman cried out.

"It's okay, momma, I got 'em! He'll get home safe and sound. I promise." The man called out to the woman below. He then looked at Goldie.

"You know, you seem so sure about a situation that you don't have any fucking control of!" Goldie told him.

"Oh, there are two things that I'm sure of, homeboy." The man began. "One, lil' dude is going home to his mother tonight and, two, your ass isn't leaving off this roof alive."

"You sure about that, Fear?" he smiled devilishly and licked the top row of his shiny gold grill.

Fear, the man with the gun, looked down at Zachary. The kid gave him a slight nod and he looked back up at Goldie.

Fear looked him square in the eyes grinning, he said, "Positive."

"Aaahhhhhh!" Goldie threw his head back hollering aloud and displaying all the teeth inside of his mouth. Zachary had sunk his teeth into his arm. "You lil' fuck!" he lifted his machete above his head and looked down at Zachary threateningly. He was about chop that little nigga'z head off, but then fire ripped through his elbow. "Gaahhhhh!"

Goldie dropped his machete and grabbed his bleeding elbow, looking up at Fear. He found the ex hit-man with his gun aimed at him. The next thing he knew he was taking two to the chest and then one in the forehead. His brain and blood sprayed out the back of his skull. Goldie killed over and fell back dramatically, grabbing the collar of Zachary's shirt. The boy's eyes grew big and he hollered out for help.

"Shit!" Fear tucked his gun into the small of his back and took off running in Zachary's direction. He appeared to be falling off the rooftop in slow motion to him. Fear slid across the rooftop with his hand outstretched to Zachary. Zachary and Goldie disappeared from out of his sight, vanishing from the rooftop. Fear reached over the edge of the rooftop and grabbed Zachary's hand. The weight of the boy jerked his arm downward.

Schriiiip!

Goldie snagged on Zachary's shirt and ripped it clean off his back. He continued to fall until he disappeared into the shadows below. His body made a thud when it hit the ground.

"Uhh!" Fear pulled Zachary back upon the rooftop and checked him for wounds. He then asked him was he okay? The boy nodded and the ex hit-man patted him on his back. "Good, let's get chu down from off this rooftop."

Fear turned his back to Zachary and motioned for him to climb upon his back. Once the boy had climbed upon his back, he climbed down from off the rooftop and walked the short path to the boy's mother. She was standing among a crowd of people, including the children her son had been playing soccer in the street with. Her face was streaked with tears. She appeared to be filled with joy to see her son. Fear let the boy down from off his back and he ran over to his mother. Rising back to his feet, Fear watched the mother and her son hug lovingly.

"Oh, thank you, thank you so much." She cried to Fear, rubbing his arm and then kissing him on the cheek.

Fear cracked a grin and continued down the path. He'd almost reached the end of it when he saw the driver. He was holding an AK-47 up at his shoulder and dragging someone.

Upon further inspection Fear realized it was Goldie's dead body. The ex hit-man put some pep in his step, eager to reach the dead man. Once he finally made it upon him, he studied his facial expression. The son of a bitch looked like he'd died in shock and excruciating agony.

"You got 'em, you got that mothafucka." The driver, Savoy, smiled and touched fists with him. "Can you believe it? Twenty-two years of tracking this piece of shit and we finally got 'em."

"Yeah, we finally got that ass." Fear replied, eyes glued on Goldie's dead face.

"I'm gonna chop his head off and keep it as a trophy. This war will be talked about for centuries. I'll have this bastard's head on my mantle when I'm old and gray, telling my grand kids about how everything went down." Savoy slung the strap of his AK over his shoulder and whipped out his machete.

He leaned down and grabbed a handful of Goldie's dreads and pulled his head upwards. He hacked at his neck until his head finally came loose. Smiling triumphantly, Savoy held the severed head up by its hair and stared into Goldie's lifeless eyes.

Nero was the crime boss and supreme ruler of all the ghettos of Brazil. He got fifty cents of every dollar that was made illegally, and if he didn't that was your ass. Having grown tired of the crime boss taxing them, Goldie's older brother, Gold Mouth, and his crew and a fraction of the criminals of Brazil joined forces to wage a war against Nero.

Nero found out about the street niggaz moving against him and had their leaders murdered.

With his brother's downfall came Goldie's rise to power. He took up his brother's cause and defeat came shortly thereafter. All of his allies were executed, forcing him to go into hiding.

Fear, who was now Nero's lead enforcer, scourged the poverty stricken streets of Rio looking for Goldie for years, but he didn't have any luck finding him. It wasn't until that night they were patrolling the slums that they spotted him coming out of a seedy motel with a whore.

Goldie was heavily armed knowing that he was a wanted man and put up one hell of a fight. Unfortunately for him, he met his end by who was said to be one of the most dangerous men to have ever picked up a gun, Alvin Simpson a.k.a Fearless.

Hearing his cellular ringing, Fear reached inside of his pocket and pulled it out. Seeing that it was Nero, he answered the call and placed the cell phone to his ear.

"'Sup?" Fear said into the cellular as he walked back towards the Toyota pickup truck.

"It's time." The caller said.

"Time?" his brows crinkled.

"Yes."

Fear's eyes instantly watered. He knew what 'It's time' meant. Those words weighed heavily on his heart, but he knew he had to face what was to come head on, like a man.

"Alright, I'll be there in a hot one." Fear disconnected the call and turned to Savoy. He found him wrapping Goldie's severed head up in the T-shirt he was wearing. The blood from the head was quickly absorbing the shirt and dripping blood into the dirt, but Savoy's crazy ass didn't seem to notice it. "It's Nero, man; we gotta hurry back to the house."

"Okay. I'm ready to go." Savoy replied.

Fear and Savoy returned to the Toyota and fled back to Nero's place.

****

Urrrrrk!

The Toyota halted outside of Nero's mansion and Fear jumped out, leaving the passenger door open behind him. With two quick bounds he was up the steps and at the double doors of the estate, pulling the door open. As soon as he crossed the threshold he found Nero's men crowding the staircase. They were discussing something with the OG's butler, Reginald, when he came inside. All of them looked to Fear as he approached, breathing heavily with glassy eyes.

The men split like The Red Sea as Fear walked through him. He stopped before Reginald and looked up at him.

"Is he…" Fear didn't have the courage to finish what he wanted to ask, but he knew that Reginald would understand what he was asking him.

"He's still with us. You can go up to see him now, if you'd like." Reginald whipped out his handkerchief and wiped his dripping eyes.

"Alright," Fear patted Reginald on his shoulder on his way up the staircase. As he climbed the staircase tears slid down his cheeks. In fact, the closer he got to Nero's master bedroom the more teardrops fell from the brims of his eyes.

Fear stepped before the double doors of Nero's bedroom and wiped his eyes with the sleeve of his shirt. He then sniffled and took a deep breath. He didn't want Nero to see him so vulnerable. He was a man of great strength and perseverance, just like him. Fear bowed his head and shut his eyelids briefly. He ran his hand down his face and took another breath. Having gathered his wits, he lifted his fist and rapped on the door.

***

A much older and withered Nero lay in bed underneath the covers. His face was pale and wrinkled. Liver spots covered his hands and some where even on his balding scalp which had strands of silver hair. The crime boss of Brazil was on his death bed due to his old age. He managed to dodge the penitentiary and assassination during his stent in the streets and he was grateful. A lot of niggaz in the life wasn't as fortunate as him. They got everything that came with the street life, unfortunately. The way Nero saw it everyone in the underworld knew what they'd signed up for so they had to accept everything that came with it.

Knock! Knock! Knock! Knock!

"Come in." Nero tried his best to sit up to address whoever was coming inside of his bedroom.

THE DEVIL WEARS TIMBS VI

A second later, one of the large double doors of Nero's bedroom opened and Fear hurried inside, shutting the door behind him. He sped walked over to the crime boss' bed and sat down beside him, placing his hand on top of his hand.

"I came as soon as I got the call. How are you doing?" Fear asked the man that had grown to be like a father to him.

"I've seen better days, son." Nero answered. "These old bones of mine are exhausted and need to rest."

"Come on now, Nero, don't talk like that. I know you gotta 'least another hunnit years left in you." He smirked and tried his best to lighten up the mood.

"Nah, I definitely don't have another hundred in me. It's my time, son, and I can't complain." Nero assured him. "I've seen it all and I've done it all, twice."

Fear looked away because he could feel himself on the verge of crying. This would be the third time he'd lost a man in his life that he loved and admired. First, it was his father, then it was his Master, and now it would Nero.

Fear batted the tears in his eyes away and looked back to Nero, saying, "I feel what chu saying, OG. I just wish I could have you here just a tad bit longer with me. You know what I'm saying?" he looked into his eyes and gripped his hand, affectionately.

Holding his gaze, Nero managed a smile and said, "If I could make that happen, I most certainly would. You've become the son that I've always wanted. And I couldn't ask for a better man to leave my empire to."

"Thanks."

"You know, lying in this bed gave me time to think. It gave me time to think looooong and hard." Nero went on to tell him. "I came to the conclusion that nothing is more important and sacred than family…blood. Then I thought of the circumstances of which you left your son in…what was his name again?"

"Kingston."

"Ah, yes, young Kingston." He smiled. "It's only right that your boy knows who his father is, and what he's about. Your blood deserves to know who his biological father is. Now, the man whose care you left him in may be an honorable fellow, but he isn't you. Kingston is *your* child."

"My son is a grown man now. I mean, what can I offer him after all the time I've been gone away from him? He doesn't need me anymore."

"Bullshit! A man always needs his father, no matter how old he gets. No one knows this better than you." Nero gripped his hand and gave him a stern look. "Go get your boy, son."

"I will. I promise."

"Excellent." the crime boss cracked a smile and patted Fear on the cheek. The ex hit-man grinned at him. "You're a good man. It has been a pleasure to have you by my side for all of these years. I cannot think of anyone better to be my successor. I don't have any doubts in my mind that you will make me…"Nero turned his head and put his fist to his mouth and coughed, harshly. His coughing was so bad that Fear picked his glass up from the dresser and poured it halfway full with water.

Fear tried to pass Nero the glass but he held up his hand, refusing it. Seeing this, Fear placed the glass and the pitcher back on the dresser, "It's my time…he's here." Nero said as he stared up at the ceiling. Wondering what he was looking at, Fear's brows furrowed and he looked at the end of his line of vision. When he didn't see anything there he was confused.

"Who, who's here?" Fear inquired, looking back and forth between the crime boss and the ceiling. He still didn't see what the OG was talking about.

A wide eyed Nero continued to stare up at the ceiling at only what he could see. Fear shook his arm gently and then harder, but he didn't say anything. His lips peeled apart and he gave his last breath, along with his final word, "Death…" His pupils dilated and his entire body relaxed.

Fear looked up at different areas of the ceiling, hoping to see what Nero was staring at, but there wasn't anything in sight. Looking back at the corpse of his street father, he shut his eyelids and crossed himself in the sign of the holy crucifix.

Afterwards, Fear outstretched the covers and covered Nero's upper body and face with it. He looked down at him and told him he loved him. Turning towards the door, he took a breath and strolled over to the double doors of the master bedroom. When he stepped outside of the door he found the living room and staircase filled with the men he'd encountered when he first entered the mansion. As soon as the door clicked closed behind Fear they all looked up at him, wondering what he was going to say.

Fear took in all of the faces of the men. He shut his eyelids briefly and shook his head. This let everyone know that Nero had left this life for the next. Tears fell from some of the men's eyes and others crossed themselves in the sign of the holy crucifix.

"Elton." Fear called out to one of Nero's noblest men.

At that moment, a man with a shaven head and thin goatee stepped from amongst the crowd on the steps, singling himself out.

"Yes, boss?"

"Make arrangements for Nero's burial. Spare no expense. I want his funeral to be fit for a king. I'm going to be taking a leave of absence so schedule the funeral three weeks from now."

"You got it, I'll take care of everything."

"Good man." Fear patted him on his shoulder. He then looked over the men again. He didn't see who he was looking for so he decided to call him forward instead, "Hershel."

Fear's eyes searched the crowd for the man he'd called upon. A robust sixty-five year old man made his way through the crowd of the men gathered on the staircase. He was a stocky fellow with a muscular build. He had a thick nappy beard and a black patch over his eye. His face and knuckles were scarred. Upon first glance you could tell he was a man who'd been through a lot of shit in his life.

"What's on your mind, young blood?" Hershel asked, looking Fear in his face with his one good eye.

"I'm going to be taking a trip to California. I'm leaving you in charge until I return." Fear told him.

"I got chu faded."

"Alright then, hold me down." Fear dapped him up. He then hugged and dapped everyone else up, before heading to his bedroom.

He showered and took care of his hygiene. Next, he threw on a black T-shirt, jeans and cowboy boots with the spurs on them. He walked over to his closet and opened the door, turning on the light switch.

Pushing the clothes hanging on the rack aside, he looked down and found a small footlocker. He picked the foot locker up with his remaining hand and sat it on his bed. He was about to open up the locker, but then he remembered he needed the key to it. That's when he walked over to the dresser and pulled open the top drawer.

He lifted up a neatly folded stack of his under shirts in the drawer and revealed a copper key. He picked up the copper key and pushed the top drawer closed.

Fear walked over to the footlocker and opened it with the key. He lifted the lid of the locker and looked down at a sleek black mechanical hand. The hand was a prosthetic. It was equipped with latches and leather straps. Looking down at the hand in the footlocker caused a smile to spread across Fear's lips. He picked up the prosthetic hand and looked at it, closely. It gleamed below the light in the ceiling.

Fear stuck the mechanical hand into his stump and turned it, locking it into place. He then pulled down the latch on the hand and buckled its straps around his arm. In doing this, he secured his prosthetic hand onto his stump. He held his mechanical hand in front of his eyes and moved its fingers. He turned his hand from front to back, continuing to move his fingers, animatedly.

"Awww, shit. That's what I'm talking about." Fear smiled having restored the usage of his left hand.

He put the footlocker back inside of the closet and snatched his duster off the rack. He slid his arms inside of the duster and adjusted its collar. Afterwards, he grabbed his wallet and passport from out of his dresser drawer. He picked up the telephone and called up the chauffeur. The chauffeur picked up on the second ring.

"Harvey, bring the car around front. I need a ride out to the airport. Okay, thanks." Fear disconnected the call. He walked over to his bedroom door and pulled it open. He was about to turn off the light switch, but something at the corner of the dresser's mirror caught his eye. It was a picture of him, Eureka and Anton. His eyes lingered on the picture for a minute. He then took a breath and turned out the light, pulling the door shut on his way out of his bedroom.

CHAPTER TWO

It was eight-three degrees on a Sunday evening, and the sun was beating down on everyone in attendance of the funeral. Some of the mourners were wearing sun hats, shades and/ or holding umbrellas to combat the rays of the sun. Every now and again, one of the people that had come out to pay their respects would wipe their sweaty forehead with the back of their hand. The elevated temperature even had some of the folks removing their suit's jackets and throwing it over their arm. Some of the women there were fanning themselves with the obituary to keep cool.

The funeral was coming to a close so the mourners were coming up to the coffin that had been lowered into the ground. They'd either toss a scoop of dirt or a rose inside of the six feet deep ditch. At the moment, Mobay was standing in line to do one of the two with one of his hands behind him, Saxton.

"I just got word mothafuckaz hit our trucks." Saxton told Mobay in a hushed tone.

"Who?" Mobay asked in a hushed tone, eyes focused on the coffin.

"I don't know for sure, but I think ol' boy that suggested we shut down shop 'cause we were stepping on his toes by selling Hercules had something to do with it." Saxton said.

Kingston was the nigga that had hit Mobay's trucks. He added the stolen shipment of Hercules to his own stash. All of the money he'd get off the lick would be all profit being that he didn't have to pay shit for the product.

When Kingston had gotten word of Mobay's people moving Hercules, he made it his business to issue him a fair warning. He caught up with him one night while he was coming out of a restaurant.

The door of the men's room opened and Mobay's bodyguards stepped inside. They checked every stall inside of the rest room. Having seen that the area was clear, they gave their boss the signal to enter. As soon as they left out, Mobay stepped in front of one of the urinals and unzipped his slacks. He pulled out his flaccid penis and whizzed, tilting his head back. He shut his eyelids and a look of relief crossed his face. Unbeknownst to him, while he was relieving himself, a pair of booted feet stepped down from the toilet's lids from the center stall. The door opened quietly and a masked individual crept up behind Mobay. The gangsta had looked down and shook his dripping dick, when the masked man slipped a fishing line around his neck. The masked assailant pulled the line against his victim's throat and crossed his fists, forming an X out of the line. Mobay's eyes bulged and mouth stretched open. Veins bulged at his temples and forehead. He struggled to slip his fingers underneath the line that was suffocating him, but his efforts were useless.

"Gaaah!" Mobay gagged and choked. Red veins formed on his eyeballs and teardrops fell from is lower eyelids. He swung from left to right trying to shake the masked man off him, but all he did was apply more pressure to his throat. It wasn't long before the life started to slowly leave Mobay's body and he found himself weakened.

"Listen, and listen good, pops, 'cause I'm given you fair warning," the masked man began gritted his teeth. "Leave Hercules alone, you can sell pussy and whatever else in the streets, but Hercules belongs to me. That's my product. It's off

limits to everyone else. Do I make myself clear?" the assailant looked into the mirror that stretched along the wall above sinks and met Mobay's distressed face. He watched as he nodded his understanding. "Good. If I hear about chu still pushing them 'roids, I'ma puff yo' mothafucking wig out, you dig?"

"Y—yes." Mobay managed to say.

Having gotten his point across, the masked man released the line from Mobay's neck and let him drop to the floor. Down on his knees, the gangsta rubbed his neck as he coughed and spat on the linoleum. Swiftly, he pulled the .38 special from his ankle holster and rose to his feet. He pointed his revolver in every direction, looking for the bastard that had nearly killed him. It seemed as if the man had vanished into the air. He wasn't any where in sight.

Mobay found himself staring ahead at nothing as he rubbed his throat, recalling where the fishing line was wrapped around his neck.

"Boss, boss, boss," Saxton called Mobay over and over again, until he snapped back to his senses.

"What's up?" Mobay glanced over his shoulder.

"Man, where you go? I lost you there for a second?"

"Just got some shit on my mind. Now, finish what chu was saying."

"Right. Whoever this mothafucka sent to do the deed did our people dirty." He shook his head thinking about how the drivers of the trucks had been done. "The nigga chopped off the truck drivers' heads and left them on the hood of their trucks."

"Son of a bitch is the devil himself." Mobay said under his breath, shaking his head. When the dude knocked off his bodyguards and told him to stop dealing Hercules, or else, he ignored, but he was hearing him loud and clear now. The old gangsta knew that his problems weren't going away unless he stopped having his people push Hercules or killed the bastard that had become a nuisance to his business. "Look here, Saxton, I want chu to find out whoever this cocksucka is and put his ass to bed. Make that happen and I'll hand you a blank check. You can write whatever dollar amount you want on it."

Saxton smiled hearing this shit. He loved money, especially new money.

****

A long distance away upon one of the cemetery's hills sat a dull black van the size of a small school bus. It had limo tinted windows and 32 inch tires. Its chrome rims shined in the sunlight casting small colorful rainbows. Inside of the van was Anton. He was dressed in the same combat gear he wore as the hit-man formerly known as Shadow.

Anton chewed gum as he looked through the lens of his muzzled sniper rifle, which was aimed out of a small slot of the back of his van. Seeing the man whose head he wanted to pop like a pimple in his crosshairs formed a wicked smile across his lips.

"Peek-a-boo, I see you." Anton chuckled and licked his chops, biting down on his bottom lip. He adjusted the scope of the high caliber weapon for a clearer look at Mobay. Next, he settled his finger on the trigger. "This is for my brotha, Ball."

"You sure this the spot, my nigga?" Anton asked as he stared into the side view mirror. His eyes were fixated on the house that he was told someone he loved very much was holed up in.

"Yeah, I'm sure, Ant," Ball assured him as he checked the chamber of his long nose chrome revolver. He was a Mexican cat with wild hair and black bags under his eyes. His hands were partially swollen and had scabs on them. This was due to his long term heroin usage. You see, Ball grew up in the Jordan Downs projects with Anton. They ran the streets together until Anton eventually left the projects for the lavish lifestyle that contract killing provided. Once things picked up for Anton, he paid a call upon Ball, who in the streets at the time strung out on heroine. Anton took the young man under his wing and got him off drugs. Wanting to pay his best friend back, Ball insisted that he trained him to be his side kick. Figuring that he could use the help since Eureka and Tristan had left the game, Anton went on to train his homeboy. Together, they took the murder game by storm. Niggaz were eating and shit was lovely. That was until Ball fucked around and killed an innocent pregnant woman during a botched hit.

Unable to cope with what he'd done, Ball turned to heroin and eventually became strung out on it again, like he once was before. Anton tried to get his best friend help but his efforts weren't of any use.

A few years later, once Cyan had been kidnapped, Anton found himself on a guilt trip and turned to heroin himself. He and Ball were kicking it like they were in the projects, only this time they were passing time by shooting up heroin.

"Yo', you gotta be sure, I'm not tryna run up in this mothafucka and the wrong people get killed. I gotta 'nough on

my conscience. The last thing I need is some innocent lives to add to it, you feel me?"

"I got chu. And I'm sure that's where I seen those mothafuckaz take Cyan." He said as he looked into the rearview mirror at the house they were staking out. "I don't know for sure, but I think they runnin' hoes out that bitch! You know, escorts? They probably got lil' mama sellin' her young goodies and shit, against her will."

Anton's face contorted into a mask of anger and he clenched his teeth. He balled his hand into a fist and looked to the side view mirror again at the house. The thought of some bastards having his niece degrade herself so that they could line their fucking pockets infuriated him.

"If that's true, on my momma, all them niggaz up in there dead, bro...all them niggaz."

"I don't blame you, 'cause let it had been my niece, there'd be hell to pay." With that having been said, Ball popped the glove box open and took out two ski masks. He kept one mask for himself and passed the other to Anton. They pulled the masks over their faces. They then checked the Glocks they were packing and hopped out of the car. Together, they hurriedly made their way up the block, taking cautious looks over their shoulders as they moved along. Once they made it upon the porch of the house, they scanned the area. Gripping his handgun with both hands, Ball stood with his back against the side of the door. He then gave Anton the signal to kick in the front door of the house.

Boom!

Anton kicked open the door and sent a spray of splinters across the living room. Right after, he and Ball *stormed inside with their handguns, holding them like police officers. Their heads were on swivels and their guns swayed around the room. The house was in complete darkness. The only illumination was coming from the street lights which were shining in through the living room window. This casted a blue hue on the right sides of Anton and Ball. The two men's brows furrowed. They were surprised to see that all of the lights inside of the house were out. They exchanged confused expressions, and then Anton gave Ball the signal to check the bedrooms down the hallway while he covered the bedrooms upstairs. With the order given, they moved to carry out their tasks. They took five steps before they were shot with tranquilizer darts.*

Pewkt! Pewkt!

Anton and Ball winced as they were shot in the chest. Ball looked down at the dart in his chest and then back up in the direction it came from. He pointed his handgun at someone camouflaged in the shadows. He was about to open fire but he felt dizzy. His eyes rolled to their whites and his head bobbled. Ball dropped his handgun and collapsed where he stood. At this time, Anton was yanking the dart out of his own chest and dropping it to the floor. Scowling, he pointed his handgun at the person hiding in the shadows. They slowly walked forward until he could make out their face. It was an older man in a fedora and a navy blue shirt with palm trees on it. He held a tranquilizer gun down at his side. He stared Anton right in his eyes as he pointed the gun at him. For a minute, he watched him blink his eyelids and try to shake off the dizzy spell the dart had brought on.

"Right about now, you're seeing about two, three...maybe even four of me and you're wondering which one you should put a bullet in. By the time you've made up *your mind that sedative will have already shut you down."* The older man, Mobay, took a Black & Mild from behind his ear. He stuck the thin cigar into his mouth and pulled out his lighter, striking a flame. He brought the bluish yellow flame to the tip of his tobacco stick and took a couple of puffs, blowing out smoke.

Bloc! Bloc! Bloc!

Anton let off three shots, all of which missed Mobay, before he dropped his gun and fell to the floor. He landed on his side and stared up at the ceiling, blinking his eyelids trying to stay awake. As he lay there, Mobay walked up on him and stood over him, blowing smoke down into his face.

"My niece...where is she? Where's Cyan?" Anton asked, struggling to stay awake.

"Cyan?" Mobay's forehead crinkled. He then looked over his shoulder and spoke to someone. "Roberta, hit them lights for me!

A second later, the lights of the living room came on. Thirty beautiful women seemed to appear, surrounding Mobay, Anton and Ball. All of the women were either wearing their pajamas or something sexy they'd planned on wearing on their dates. These women were Mobay's whores. He was about his money. He sold heroin, crack, steroids and pussy.

"Now, I gotta few new ladies in my stable, but I'm pretty sure none of them are called Cyan. But I'm going to double check, just for you." Mobay told Anton. Keeping his eyes on him, he addressed his whores. "Are any of you ladies named Cyan or have ever been called Cyan?"

"No, Big Daddy!" the women said in unison.

"And there you have it, son."

"You're...you're lying." Anton picked up his handgun and got upon his knees. He lifted his gun and pointed it at Mobay. All of the women looked afraid, but the old man didn't look the least bit shook.

Mobay stared down at Anton for a second. Then out of the blue, he kicked the gun out of his hand and kicked him across the chin. The sharp blow knocked him out cold and sent him slamming face first into the floor.

"Alright, girls, back as you were. I'll handle this mess." Mobay told his whores. As the women went on about their business, he tucked his tranquilizer gun at the front of his pants and pulled out his cell phone. He then hit up his left and right hands, telling them where he needed them to be. Afterwards, he put his cell phone away and pulled out his tranquilizer gun again. He sat down on the couch smoking his Black & Mild and watching Anton and Ball, closely. If any one of them awoke before they were supposed to he was going to pop their ass with another tranquilizer dart.

Twenty minutes later the doorbell was chiming and Mobay was rising from off the couch to answer the door. As soon as he pulled the front door open, his bodyguards filed inside with a worn black leather bag. They went to work gagging and restraining Anton's and Ball's wrists. Right after, they were carrying them outside and tossing them into the back of the van they'd driven to the place in.

****

Anton and Ball slowly came awake from the tranquilizer darts they'd been shot with. They tried to move and that's when they noticed their wrists were bound behind their back. Hearing the radio playing, they looked up front to see two men. These were the men Mobay had called upon to take Anton and Ball off of his hands. Anton and Ball didn't know where they were being taken, but they were confident once they got there they wouldn't be heard from again.

With that in their mind, Anton and Ball sat up as quietly as they could. They then started to work themselves out of their restraints as fast as they could. Anton managed to get himself out of his restraints and pulled the gag down from out of his mouth. He went to help Ball, but he shrugged him off. He then nodded to the double doors of the van, signaling for him to get the doors open.

Anton nodded his understanding and crept over to the double doors. As he was opening the doors as gently as he could, Ball was pulling the gag down from out of his mouth. Anton slowly opened one of the double doors, but it made a squeak, alerting the niggaz that were riding up front. The nigga in the front passenger seat looked over his shoulder and saw Anton and Ball trying to escape.

"What the fuck?" he blurted and pulled out his gun.

"What's up?" the nigga behind the wheel asked, brows wrinkled.

"These mothafuckaz tryna escape!" homeboy that had pulled out his gun said. He then pointed his gun at Anton. When Anton saw the hollow barrel of the gun staring at him, his eyes bugged and he leaped out of the van. The shot that was fired missed his head by an inch.

When old boy pointed his gun at Ball he went to leap out of the back of the van too, but he wasn't fast enough. He winded up getting shot in the back and crumpling to the floor.

As soon as he went down, the nigga that shot him kicked him in the side. He then looked out of the back of the van through the door that was hanging wide open. He saw Anton tumbling down the street hastily. Angry, he popped a couple of shots at him and then slammed the door shut.

Once the nigga slammed the door shut, he tucked his gun and restrained Ball again.

"You get the other nigga that was back there?" homeboy behind the wheel asked over his shoulder, one hand on the steering wheel.

"Hell naw, man, mothafucka got away." Old boy that shot at Anton said as he gagged Ball's mouth again.

"What do we tell Mobay if he asks?"

"Shit the truth. Shit happens, hell!" old boy sat back down in the front passenger seat.

"Fuck it." Dude behind the wheel said.

His partner turned up the volume on the song currently playing on the radio and nodded his head to it.

"This my shit right here." The driver announced.

"Mine too." The nigga in the front passenger seat continued to nod his head.

Sitting in the back of the van bleeding and wincing, Ball couldn't help blaming himself for the situation he was in. He knew he was fucked because the dudes that had kidnapped him were definitely going to kill him, but he was glad that Anton had at least gotten away.

Ball had told Anton he saw Cyan going inside of the house because he knew the girls that stayed there were known to keep at least a kilo of blow deck. The girls were escorts and they often indulged in heroin and/or alcohol. Ball figured he could get Anton to raid the spot with him, and while he was busy looking for his niece, he could make off with whatever drugs he found inside of the place. What he didn't count on was their pimp being there, because had he known, he sure as hell wouldn't have run up in the place.

God, if you can hear me, please get me outta this situation. If you do, I promise I'll quit dope…forever, Ball thought to himself. He shut his eyelids and tears jetted down his cheeks, running over his mouth. The bullet in his back had him feeling like he was burning on the inside and he couldn't bare the pain.

Ball didn't know it at the time but his praying to God was useless. This would be his last time riding anywhere.

****

"Consider that fool dead and buried," Saxton said, adjusting the sleeves of his suit. All he could think about was the dollar amount he was going to write on that check Mobay was going to hand him for knocking off that pain-in-the-ass that had hit his shipment of Hercules.

"Gemme a sec, will ya?" Mobay told him, feeling his cell phone vibrate within the confines of his suit's jacket. He wasn't going to answer his cellular, but then he remembered he was looking for a very important business call. Mobay switched hands with the rose he was holding and reached inside of his suit to pull out his cell phone.

THE DEVIL WEARS TIMBS VI

He'd almost pulled his cellular completely out when it slipped from his hand. He cursed under his breath seeing his cell fall at his feet. As soon as he went to bend down to pick it up, Saxton was visible behind him. Right there on the spot, Saxton's forehead exploded. Bloody goo and brain fragments went flying in every direction and his limp body fell to the ground.

The screams and panic hollers of men, women and children filled the air. People were running back and forth across the lawn, heads ducked to avoid catching a bullet.

Lying where he was on the ground, Mobay looked up and saw the van upon the hill. He called out to all of the men in attendance that'd drawn their guns as soon as Saxton's head exploded, telling them where he believed the sniper was. Just then, the bulletproof limousine that Mobay had been chauffeured to the cemetery in pulled into the line of vision of the sniper, ruining the killa'z shot.

Thankful there was something between him and the sniper, Mobay scrambled over to the center of the limo. Reaching inside of his suit's jacket, he pulled out his gun and peered through the passenger window. Through the window he saw the van he was sure the sniper was picking niggaz off from. Looking to his men, Mobay gave them the signal to engage whomever it was trying to take him out.

As soon as Mobay pointed in the direction the shot was fired from, his men and a band of others went in the direction of the van. They pulled out their handguns and ran towards the van. They got halfway to the van before taking shots at it. Their bullets deflected off the bulletproof vehicle and went flying in different directions. Seeing that the rounds from their weapons weren't penetrating the van, the men continued to charge forward, busting their guns. One after another, the sniper started picking their asses off, with headshots, busting their domes like puss filled zits.

****

Anton picked off one more of the men coming at him and then sat his murder weapon down. Next, he walked over to a smaller armored vehicle and unlocked it. He lifted its door and sat down in the driver's seat, shutting the door once he'd strapped himself in.

****

The niggaz that were busting on the van surrounded it and opened fire on it, but their bullets only left scratches behind.

"This shit bulletproof or somethin'!" One of the men claimed.

Ka-Boom

The back double doors of the van flung outward and a jet black motor vehicle with tinted windows sped out. It ripped down the grassy hill leaving pieces of grass in its wake it was going so fast. Mobay's men started to go after the vehicle, but the van suddenly exploded. Smoke, flames and large shrapnel went flying everywhere.

"Gahhhh!"

"Ahhhhhh!"

"Rahhhhhh!"

"Graaahhhh!"

Mobay's men hollered out in agony as shrapnel went halfway through their torsos and stuck out of their backs. Their blood quickly expanded on their button-down shirts and the upper half of their suit's jackets. The men eventually fell to their deaths. Those of them that weren't dead were critically wounded from smaller pieces of shrapnel and eventually bled to death.

Vroooom!

The motor vehicle sped down the hill. Anton looked into the side view mirror and saw some other niggaz that were attending the funeral running upon the hill. They looked like shadowy figures from the distance he was. The fools that were attending the funeral lifted their guns and pointed them at the motor vehicle, pulling their triggers.

Blocka! Blocka! Blocka! Boc! Boc! Poc! Poc! Poc!

Splocka! Splocka! Splocka! Bloc! Bloc! Bloc! Bloc!

Sparks flew off the motor vehicle as bullets deflected off its bulletproof exterior. Once the last bullet bounced off of the vehicle, its spoiler lifted up and two gun barrels rose up. The barrels extended and swiveled as they opened fire. Howls of pain came from the men that were busting on Anton's vehicle. Bullets pelted their torsos and turned their suits crimson. One after another they fell to the grassy hill, still holding their guns. Once the guns of Anton's vehicle ceased their firing they enveloped back inside of their hiding place. Right after, the spoiler came back into its rightful place

Vroooom!

Anton turned off the grassy hill onto the paved ground and ripped up the path. The exit of the cemetery was growing closer and closer the further he got to it. Just then, police cars spilled through the exit and zoomed in his direction.

A compartment on the right and left side of Anton's vehicle opened and miniature .50 caliber machine guns emerged. The machine guns vibrated as they spat ammunition and blew large holes in the police cars. The windshields of some of the police cars cracked into cobwebs, some of their hoods flew off and some of their tires burst. Some of the police cars experienced all of the above.

Having dispatched the oncoming police cars, the machine guns returned to their hiding places. Next, another police car sped inside of the cemetery, flying towards Anton. Another compartment opened on Anton's vehicle's left side and a small missile came into play. It moved at different angles until it locked onto the police car. Before Anton could fire the missile at the oncoming police car, one of the damaged police cars crashed into him. The impact caused his smaller vehicle to tumble until it landed on its rooftop. It lay where it landed wrecked and smoking. The police officers hopped out of their cars and drew their guns. They slowly moved in on Anton's vehicle from all angles.

Every dog has his day.

CHAPTER THREE

That night

The police officer, a stocky built Mexican cat with a buzz cut walked a sickly looking Anton towards the holding cell. As he was walking him along his cellular rung and vibrated. He allowed the cell phone to ring and it eventually stopped. Once it started up again, he smacked his lips and rolled his eyes, wondering who in the hell was blowing up his jack while he was at work. Figuring that it was an emergency, he pulled out his cellular. Seeing the number across the display made his forehead crease. He answered the device and placed it to his ear.

"Yeah. I got 'em right now, takin' 'em to the holdin' cell." He said, and then listened to what he was being told. "That's one tall fuckin' order, considerin' there's cameras all over this place. How much? Nah, nah, nah, I can do it. Just lemme putta call in to my buddy, give 'em a heads up. Alright, meet me around back in the alley in thirty minutes." He disconnected the call and stashed his cell phone. "Great news, asshole, someone just bought you a get outta jail free card."

"Oh, really? Be sure to thank your mother for me." Anton cracked with a smirk.

With that having been said, the officer tightened the handcuffs around his wrists, causing him to wince. "Come on, smart ass." The officer handled Anton roughly as he turned him around and led him in the opposite direction. Heading back up front, the officer gave one of his buddies in the precinct a signal, which he picked up on quickly. He wanted him to kill the surveillance cameras. Homeboy gave him a nod and set his cup of coffee down on his desk top to handle the task appointed to him.

Crooked shit wasn't anything new between these two badges. These mothafuckaz worked for whoever dropped a bag on them. They didn't give a fuck. Just as long as that money was green and printed in the United States of America, they were going to get it, by any means necessary.

****

The police officer led Anton through the backdoor of the precinct into the alley. It was here that they found two shining white orbs and heard the low humming of an engine. As soon as Anton's eyes met the illumination of the headlights he narrowed his eyelids into slits and turned his head. The police officer went to move him forward and he vomited, splashing what looked like greenish pink goop with chunks of food in it on the ground.

"Gotdammit!" the officer frowned up and moved his pattern leather boot back before it could get soiled. "You almost got that shit on my boots."

"Man, fuck them boots, I'm sick! I need some dope." Anton said, looking sickly with goo dripping from his mouth. His eyes were hooded and he looked like he was about to collapse, breathing funny.

"You fucking junkie! Getting your next fix is the least of your problems." the officer said as he ushered Anton towards the Lincoln Town Car awaiting him in the alley. "Do you know who you ran afoul of? Mobay. Mobay is one mean motor scooter."

"Why you holding that man's dick, bruh? You think he's the only killa out here? Shiiiiit, I been knocking niggaz' heads off since I was fifteen. You better ask about me." Anton rasped, looking exhausted from throwing up.

"Yeah, well, none of that shit is going to matter once Mobay gets his hands on you."

"My nigga, you focused on what's gone happen to me, when you need to be worrying about that broken nose and them aching balls."

The officer's face scrunched up and he said, "What broken nose and aching ba…"

The rest of the words died in the law enforcer's throat when Anton swung his head back with all his might. The force behind the blow busted the officer's nose and sent blood spraying from his nostrils. He went to grab his face and, Anton, without turning around, slammed the heel of his boot into his crotch. The officer howled in pain and grabbed his privates. Anton jumped over his shackled wrists, which put his handcuffs in the front of him instead of behind his back. He then did a spin-kick, launching the heel of his boot against the officer's jaw and spilling him to the ground.

Anton looked down at the officer who was lying on his back, bloody and battered. The man moaned in pain and his eyelids fluttered. Seeing he'd dispatched the law enforcer, Anton took off running down the alley towards the Lincoln Town Car. In motion, he saw the driver's door open and a man in a black suit step out. The man held a mask of seriousness and gripped his gun. Holding it with both hands, he pointed the weapon and opened fire.

Atoms of concrete flew up into the air at Anton's feet as he charged at the man licking shots at him. He leaped high up into the air and the man lifted his gun, firing at him continuously. The bullets whizzed past Anton, missing him. Using the flying bullets to his advantage, he brought the chain of his handcuffs towards them. Sparks flew as a bullet went through the chain of his handcuffs and severed them. Anton flipped over in the air with bullets still flying around him. He came down and kicked the man in his chest so hard that he flew backwards and his gun went up into the air.

The man that was licking shots at Anton hit the ground on his back, hard. Anton took off running down the alley like he had the devil on his heels. By this time, the front passenger door of the Lincoln Town Car opened and another man in a black suit hopped out with a gun. He pointed his weapon down the alley and opened fire, missing. Once he saw that Anton had gotten too far down the alley, he holstered his gun and jumped back inside of the Lincoln Town Car. As he was jumping back inside the whip, the other man in the black suit scrambled to his feet and picked up his gun. He ran over to the Lincoln Town Car and jumped back behind the wheel. He threw the vehicle in *reverse* and mashed the gas pedal. The automobile went flying backwards, lighting up the other half of the alley with its back lights.

"Haa! Haa! Haa! Haa! Haa!" Anton ran down the alley occasionally looking over his shoulder, and seeing the Lincoln Town Car getting closer and closer. Sweat dripped off his brow and his heart raged in his chest. "Shit, these mothafuckaz coming!"

Anton bowed his head and ran as hard as he could, gritting his teeth. Still, the Lincoln Town Car was gaining in on him, closing the distance between them.

Bump!

The back of the Lincoln slammed into Anton and he crashed to the asphalt. He lay where he was on the side of his face, wincing. As he was struggling to get up, the Lincoln stopped behind him, the back lights shined on the back of him. The men in the black suits jumped out of the vehicle and made their way towards Anton. Stopping on either side of him, they proceeded to stomp and kick the shit out of him.

"Hold him up, hold him up against the fucking wall!" the officer that Anton had knocked out speed walked down the alley. He drew his nightstick from off his side and motioned with his finger for the men in suits to put Anton's ass against the wall. Once they did, he walked over to him and slammed the nightstick into his gut, twice. He then struck Anton across his jaw. When he stepped back after busting his grill, he watched him spit blood on the ground. The officer smiled wickedly at what he'd done. He then proceeded to beat the hell out of Anton.

While the officer was giving Anton a beating, the back door of the Lincoln Town Car opened and Mobay stepped out. He shut the back door behind him and leant against the side of the vehicle he was chauffeured to the location in. He took casual pulls of his cigar as he watched Anton being assaulted. When Anton looked up at who had gotten out of the Lincoln, the only thing he could see was the ember tip of the cigar and the lower half of his suit. This was due to the darkness of the alley partially hiding him.

Wop!

The officer cracked Anton upside his skull and he fell at his feet unconscious. Looking down at his victim, the officer spat on him and then kicked him in his side. He then wiped his bleeding nose with the back of his fist. Seeing the blood smeared on his knuckles, he kicked him once again and cursed him out. Feeling someone at his back, the officer turned around to find Mobay handing him a hefty envelope. The officer smiled and sheathed the nightstick. He then took the envelope and opened it, satisfied with the cash he found inside. Afterwards, he shook Mobay's hand and stashed the envelope inside of his jacket. Mobay patted the officer on his shoulder as he walked passed him, heading back towards the precinct.

"Bound this piece of shit's wrists and ankles and put 'em inside of the trunk." Mobay ordered the men in black as he stared down at Anton. On his command, the men in black did what they were told and dumped Anton inside of the trunk. A minute later the Lincoln Town Car drove off down the alley.

****

Anton sat duct-taped to an iron chair inside of a dark basement. A chain linked light bulb dangled above his head putting him in the spot light and exposing the damage that had been done to him. Anton had a large lump on his forehead, an eye that was swollen shut and busted lips. Several cuts littered his face. The bleeding of the cuts ran down his neck and soiled the collar of his white undershirt pink.

Anton's head was bowed and his chest expanded and compressed with each breath he took. Mobay's men, which were the cats in the black suits, were now in button-down shirts. Their shirts were stained with dots of blood from them punching on Anton for the past half hour. They'd take turns beating him. When one of them would get tired, the other would take his turn. They would go back and forth. That was until Mobay called them off. If the old man hadn't done this, then his men would have surely beaten Anton to death.

"You want me to finish 'em off, Mr. Powell?" one of the men asked as he gripped his holstered handgun. The moment his boss gave him the word he was going to put one right through Anton's dome.

"Nah, let 'em breathe for a few ticks. I want 'em to see what I had done to his little Spic friend." Mobay dropped his cigar at his feet and mashed it out under his hard bottom shoe.

He stepped before Anton and reached inside of his suit, pulling out a cellular phone. He gave the man he was talking to earlier a nod and he grabbed Anton by his hair, yanking his head back. Anton winced feeling a sharp pain rip through his scalp. With his one good eye he observed Mobay and wondered what was going through his head at the time.

Once Mobay found the footage on the cell phone he was looking for, he turned the screen to Anton so he could watch it.

"I want him to watch it all," Mobay told the man that was going to blow Anton's head off a minute ago. "If his narrow-ass so much as bat's an eye, you send him to the Most High."

"With pleasure," He drew his holstered handgun and pressed it against the side of Anton's head. An evil smile spread across his lips as he hoped and prayed Anton defied his boss' orders so he could make good on the command he was given.

Looking at the display of the cell phone, Anton found a battered and bloodied Ball standing on the balls of his bare feet. There was blood at his toes. His arms were outstretched and bound by chains which were wrapped around pillars inside of a basement. Anton's brows furrowed and familiarity struck him like a punch to the gut. His head whipped from left to right seeing the same pillars in the basement he was in. He looked down and saw splatters of blood at his feet. The basement he was inside of was indeed the very same one that his homeboy, Ball had been tortured in.

THE DEVIL WEARS TIMBS VI

"Let me confirm it for you," Mobay started, garnering Anton's full attention. "That little wetback bastard died in the very same space you're sitting in."

Hearing what he was thinking confirmed, Anton growled and clenched his fists. He wanted to leap out of his chair and get in Mobay's ass, but he feared his brain would be flying across the room before he'd gotten the chance to put his hands on him. Although he was courageous, he wasn't a fucking fool. The way he saw it, if he could live past the day, he would someday get his revenge.

"Watch it!" Mobay demanded he watch the footage on the cell phone's screen. Anton mad dogged him, keeping his hateful eyes on the gangsta standing before him. He defied him openly. "I said, 'watch it before I have my man nod your punk-ass!'"

With the threat having been laid down, Anton directed his eyes back on the display of the cell phone. At this point in the footage, Ball's head was bowed and blood was dripping from his forehead. Mobay, who was standing aside wearing goggles, a black leather smock and dish washing gloves, gripped a chainsaw. He gave the cord of the old machine two good tugs before it buzzed to life. The spiked metal chain outlining the lengthy blade spun intensely. The sound of the blade ripped through the air, squealing annoyingly.

Hearing the deathly sound of the chainsaw, Ball slowly began to regain consciousness. His head bobbed about and his eyelids twitched. The closer the sound of the chainsaw came to him, the further his eyelids stretched open. Once his vision came into focus and he saw the buzzing blade of the chainsaw, Ball struggled to get off the chains that bound his wrists. When that didn't work, he threw his head back and tried to holler out for help. Unfortunately for him, the duct tape that was stretched across his mouth blocked any sound from escaping his lips.

Mobay brought the blade of the chainsaw above Ball's kneecaps. The spiked metal blade ripped through the flesh, ligaments and bones of his legs, spraying blood everywhere. As the blade went through Ball's legs his eyes rolled to their whites and he shook uncontrollably, going into shock. Once his severed bloody limbs fell to the floor, Mobay brought the chainsaw across Ball's neck. Blood sprayed Mobay in the face and he shook it off, as he continued to remove his victim's head. Once Ball's head smacked down on the surface, Mobay went ahead and removed both of his arms. Once he did, Ball's torso dropped to the floor along with his shackled arms. The chainsaw continued to buzz loudly and annoyingly, until its welder eventually cut it off.

The recording stopped and Mobay tucked the cellular where he'd pulled it out from. He then looked to Anton whose eyes had slightly watered. He watched as he squeezed his eyelids tight and then opened them. The tears in his eyes were gone and replaced with hatred. He looked up at Mobay with unforgiving eyes.

"I've seen worse, mothafucka, try again!" Anton spat. His smart-ass mouth caused Mobay to scowl and clench his jaws. The gangsta thought for sure that seeing his friend hacked up would have Anton begging for mercy, but that wasn't the case. What he didn't know was Anton was of a different breed. For lack of a better phrase, *He Was Built For The Shit.* What kind of shit, you ask? That gangsta shit!

Whack!

Homeboy holding the gun to Anton's head smacked him upside his dome with it. The impact from the weapon launched his head forward. His head hung and he threw it back, wincing. Dude that smacked Anton upside his crown with his gun pointed it back at his head. He looked back and forth between Anton and Mobay. He was eager to pull the trigger but he wouldn't go through with it unless his boss gave him the nod to do so.

"Lemme do this mothafucka, Mr. Powell, please. Please, I'm begging you." The man said, clenching his jaws. He was so anxious to bust Anton's head that his dick was hard.

Mobay and Anton locked eyes, staring one another down. The intensity shared between them was so thick you could cut it with a knife. Even with the odds stacked against him, Anton didn't show fear or nervousness. He was as solid as a rock, and ready to face whatever the gangsta had in store for him.

"Just gemme the word, boss, and I'ma give this nigga his wings." The man kept looking back and forth between Anton and his employer. His trigger finger was itching and he was dying to put another notch under his belt.

Mobay lifted his hand and said, "Be easy, let the little nigga breathe. I like him…I like him a lot. That's the only reason why I'm going to let him keep his life."

"Keep his life?" Mobay's men, the ones that had been beating the living shit out of Anton said in unison. They couldn't believe their ears. They just knew that their boss was going to grant Anton's ass his Death Wish. They were sadly mistaken though.

Mobay's eyebrows arched and he looked between his two flunkies, saying, "Did I stutter, mothafuckaz? Y'all niggaz heard me. I'm not in the habit of repeating shit, especially when I know all parties involved clearly heard my ass. Now, I said the man gets to keep his life, and that's that."

The man took the gun from Anton's head and stuck it back inside of its holster. Looks of disappointment crossed him and his partner-in-crime faces. They were looking forward to catching a body, but their desires would have to be put on hold that night.

Having seen his men obey his command, Mobay focused his attention back on Anton who was still eyeballing him. Seeing that he had his undivided attention, he went on to address him, "Look here, homie, I am going to let chu keep your life, but it's going to cost you. It's not going to be cheap, either. In fact, it's gone run you about fifty stacks. I'm going to need that cheddar, Asap. I'm talking tonight. I don't give a fuck what chu got to do to get it, but my ass had better have a bag sitting before me by the time given. Is that understood?" Anton didn't say anything. He continued mad dogging the gangsta, thinking of all the ways he'd like to kill him. Feeling disrespected by his lack of an answer, Mobay snatched the holstered gun that was in his man's possession and pressed it against Anton's forehead. To Mobay's surprise, Anton didn't even flinch. "Like I explained to my guys here, I am not in the habit of repeating myself…to anyone. This includes you."

Anton continued to stare down Mobay for a minute before finally answering him, "Understood."

"Good, boy," Mobay flipped the gun around so that the barrel would be in his hand. He then outstretched the weapon towards his flunky. The man took the gun and holstered it. "Cut his bondages and escort him to the car." Mobay ordered his men. After he gave them his command, he told Anton where to deliver the money and headed up the staircase to get into his Lincoln Town Car.

Once Mobay was out of sight, the man that had holstered his gun turned to Anton and punched him in the chin. He fell over in the chair knocked out cold. For good measure, the man kicked Anton in the stomach. Afterwards, he removed his bondages with a switch blade from his back pocket. Him and his partner then hoisted him up by his arms and dragged him up the basement staircase.

CHAPTER FOUR

A twenty-five-year-old Kingston stood before his dresser's mirror as naked as the day he was born, taking in his appearance. He was a solid six foot one and had a dark caramel complexion. He rocked his hair in a temple fade which swirled with deep waves. His goatee was thin and led down to a thick bush of chin hair. The young man's muscular physique and tattoo covered body gave him the appearance of a gangsta rapper.

The nigga had more markings on him than a New York underground subway. *Anton* was on one side of his neck, *Tristan* was on the other, *Bootsy* was on the back of his left arm, above his elbow, and *Cyan* was behind his right ear. He also had *Giselle* on the back of his right wrist.

His mother, *Eureka,* was on his right peck, the Watts Tower was on his left peck and .45 handguns were on either side of his navel.

On his right arm there was a pair of construction Timberland boots hanging from a phone line, and beneath them was *The Devil Wears Timbs.* On his hand, between his thumb and finger was *L.O. E,* which meant *Loyalty Over Everything.* Across his broad shoulders was *Rest In Paradise, Nasir.* This was the child that Constance would have had by Fear, but unfortunately he did not make it. Below this tattoo was a coffin with a crucifix on it. On one side was the birth date of the child and on the other was the death date. Below the coffin was *Gone But Never Forgotten.*

Like his father before him, Kingston was an academic genius who just so happened to be born into money. He was drawn to the streets, and the celebrity, money, bitches and power they brought. The streets had a hold on the boy like a pimp had on his whore. Although Tristan and Eureka pushed him to finish his education after high school, he rebelled against them. The street life was far too appealing, and he couldn't get enough of it.

Kingston's decision led to him spending time between his suburban neighborhood and the places his mother and father grew up, which was the Eastside of South Central Los Angeles (The Low Bottomz) and The Eastside of Watts, in the Jordan Downs Projects. It was these places that he earned his bones hustling, knocking niggaz out and busting on everything moving that had a problem with the cats that were standing on the same side of the line that he was.

The homies in Watts and the Low Bottomz had mad respect and love for Kingston, so he claimed them both as his own. Unlike his father, Fear, he didn't bang Blood, but he didn't bang Crip either. His bonds with his homies were so strong that he remained neutral. It didn't matter though, because mothafuckaz knew he'd bust his guns if he had to, and even if he didn't, he had an army of riders at his disposal that wouldn't hesitate to kill on his behalf.

Kingston tried his hand at contract killing, like the rest of his family. He took out hits on mid level players, informants and witnesses. He found out rather quickly that the teachings of his uncle Anton gave him an unfair advantage over any enemies his employers saw fit to sic him on. The poor bastards that had befallen victim to his gun didn't stand a chance.

Eventually Kingston grew tired of the murder for hire game. He found himself with the itch to get money. I'm talking about real money, the kind that couldn't be made working a 9 to 5 at some commercial fast food joint. The hustle was in the boy's veins, and rightfully so, before his father was the merciless killa that he was today, he was a crack king, pushing poison to the lost souls of the ghetto.

Kingston wasn't a stranger to hustling. He'd sold everything from weed to heroin. Hell, if it could be sold in the streets then he could sell it, and make one hell of a profit off of it too. Anyway, he got himself a plug on a steroid called Hercules. Now Hercules wasn't like any other steroid on the underground market. The drug could enhance an individual's physical capabilities, instantly. Although they could, the user didn't have to take the drug while working out to gain results. No, they could take Hercules and get their results right there on the spot. This was why the drug was so popular. Its market value could make someone rich overnight, and that's exactly what the drug did for Kingston.

When Kingston started slinging Hercules there were a few cats in Southern California with their hands already on the stuff. He knew that in order for him to become the go-to-man that he had to make it so that he was the only mothafucka with the shit for sell. So he made it his business to find out exactly who the other drug dealers were that was distributing the infamous steroid. As soon as he did he made sure all of those mothafuckaz met with death.

As a result of him and his hittas laying their murder game down, Kingston's profit went through the roof, seemingly overnight. The young nigga was sitting on bags…big bags. So much so, that his last drop offs were going to be made tonight. After that, he was going to turn the field work over to his street soldiers. The way he saw it, he was a young boss, so what the fuck did he look like making moves on the streets getting his hands dirty? Nah, that's why he now had soldiers at his disposal. He'd pay them to do the dirty work while his hands stayed clean and he called the shots from a far…just like his daddy use to.

"You talking about Constance?" Kingston looked back at the woman he'd finished sexing not long ago, pressing his finger against the tattoo on his forearm. They'd been conversing about the ink on his body. The broad he was having the discussion with was a youthful looking white woman with fire engine red hair. She had tits and ass that were perfect for her curvaceous body. She nodded yes to his question and took another pull from her cancer stick, blowing smoke up into the air. "Constance was my pops ride or die. She was the definition of a down ass bitch, you feel me?"

"She was his girlfriend, right?" Wendy, the naked Caucasian woman asked, as she leaned over and tapped her square, dumping ashes into the ashtray on the dresser.

"Nah, not his girlfriend," He went on to explain. "You see, my old man was a hit-man and a jack boy. He rescued Constance from some sex traffickers or some shit, like that. Anyway, she felt indebted to my pops and wanted to repay 'em. She begged 'em to train her to be a killa like him, and at first he wasn't fucking with her. But eventually, he put her down with 'em and gave her the game."

"What about that one on your shoulder? Italia."

"Now, that was my pops fiancée." He told her. "She was down for 'em as well. From what I was told by my moms, she was what any and every man wanted in his woman. My pops loved her, which meant a lot, because from what I understand, my pops had never loved any woman…besides my moms, of course."

"Is she still alive?"

"Nah," he shook his head no. "She got whacked by Constance…behind my old man. See, Constance was a nutcase when it came to my pops. She couldn't see anyone being with 'em besides her, so she killed Italian so she could have my pops all to herself."

"Wow!" her eyelids stretched wide open and she sat further up in bed, still smoking her cigarette.

"What?" his brows furrowed as he wondered what was on her mind.

"You have two women on you. One of which was killed by the other over your father. Now, one would think you'd have one but not the other."

"True." He nodded his understanding. "But all of the women that are inked on me have one thing in common, and it's 'cause of that one thing," he wagged the one finger he had held up. "That I've shown my respect by honoring them with their names inked on my flesh."

"Oh yeah, why's that?"

"Their undying loyalty to my father."

"Humph," she nodded as she stared out at nothing. The cigarette she had wedged between her fingers wafted with smoke.

Taking a deep breath, Kingston turned around to her, "Anyway, that's enough for story time. Gone and wash up, I'll call you an Uber. I gotta few moves I needa make."

"Alright, Big Daddy," Wendy grinned as she mashed out her cigarette and threw the sheets from off her. She then hopped her naked-ass up and walked towards the bathroom, smacking Kingston on his left buttock along the way. Kingston watched as his fuck-buddy sauntered her happy ass inside of the bathroom and shut the door behind her. A moment later, he heard shower water running inside of the tub.

Kingston couldn't help thinking of how he loved his arrangement with Wendy. Not only was she his quote unquote 'therapist', she was his whore for that night. He paid her handsomely for her services. And although they had been dealing with one another for quite some time, there were absolutely no romantic feelings involved between them. Kingston was fine with that. He wouldn't have it any other way; because with the life he led he didn't have time for dating or a serious relationship.

Kingston put on some gray sweatpants and walked inside of his walk-in closet. He flipped on the light switch and made a beeline over to a rack of clothing. He slid the clothing aside and revealed a digital safe. He placed his palm down against the hand impression on the side of the safe. The impression turned green and the storage unit beeped, unlocking. Kingston pulled open the safe and revealed pill bottles and vials of Hercules. He grabbed a small leather bag from out of the safe and began placing some of the steroids inside of it. Once he was done, he zipped the bag up and shut the safe. He sat the bag down on the table at the center of the closet. Right after, he clapped his hands sporadically and Money Man's *Boss Up* erupted from the speakers placed in the upper corners of the walk-in closet.

> *I had to boss up for a check*
>
> *I had to step on these niggas neck*
>
> *I had to go and get a couple stripes*

THE DEVIL WEARS TIMBS VI

I had to trap all day and night

I remember those cold nights

I hit it like I just got out da pen

I bought a brick and I go get it in

As the music played Kingston looked through his clothing to find something to wear that night.

Missing person flyers with Cyan Teretto's face on them were posted on every light pole, telephone pole, telephone booth, mail box and building in the city. In fact, you couldn't go anywhere without seeing the missing person flyer. You couldn't escape them. They were everywhere. Hell, the flyers combined with the advertisement running on television every so often guaranteed that if someone had seen Cyan Teretto, she'd already be home right now, but unfortunately that wasn't the case.

A missing person flyer with Cyan's face on it hung on by its corner on a telephone pole at the corner. The cool breeze that occasionally brushed against it caused it to flap, but it refused to be snatched from where it had been stapled. In the distance a speeding car could be heard. The sound of its engine getting louder and louder the closer it came. The red stoplight had just turned green when a Honda Accord ripped through the intersection.

Vrooooom!

The force of the wind from the vehicle speeding past the corner snatched the missing person's flyer from the telephone pole. The flyer went high up into the air and slowly descended back towards the ground.

THE DEVIL WEARS TIMBS VI

Forty-five minutes later

Tyjuan sat behind the wheel of his navy blue Tahoe truck with the deep dish chrome rims. He nodded his head to Future's *Fuck up some commas* while drumming his fingers on the steering wheel. Occasionally, he'd find himself glancing up in the rear view mirror to see if the cat he was meeting that night had pulled up or not. When he didn't see him, he went back to nodding his head to the music and eventually started spitting some of the lyrics.

Let's fuck up some commas, nigga (Let's fuck up some commas)

Hunnit thousand, to five hunnit thousand, five hunnit thousand....

Knock! Knock! Knock! Knock!

A rap at the front passenger window startled Tyjuan. He nearly jumped out of his seat. He was about to pull off until he looked and found his plug standing hunched over at the window. This put him at ease because he knew that it was homeboy that he linked up with every month to get his medication, as he liked to call it. Tyjuan popped the locks on his vehicle and Kingston pulled open the door. He slid into the front passenger seat and slammed the door shut behind him. He then reached inside of his leather jacket and pulled out an orange pill bottle, handing it to Tyjuan. After taking the bottle, Tyjuan went to hold it up to get a better look at its contents, but Kingston grabbed him by his wrist. The young nigga looked around cautiously to make sure there weren't any eyes watching them.

"What's up? Why you trippin'?" Tyjuan's brows furrowed, wondering why homeboy had grabbed him roughly.

"Trippin'? Nigga, I'm not tryna be locked up fighting a federal drug charge on the account of yo' mothafucking ass not knowing how to be incognito. Fuck that! You know our arrangement. We make the same exchange every month, ain't shit changed. It's the same thirty pills in that bottle as it was the last time."

"How much?" he looked back and forth between the pill bottle and Kingston.

Kingston, feeling himself getting heated, bowed his head and massaged the bridge of his nose. Suddenly, Tyjuan started busted up laughing, causing him to look at him with a crinkled forehead. "I'm fuckin' with chu, G. Hold up," he switched hands with the pill bottle and stuck his hand inside of his basketball shorts, pulling out a thick wad of dead presidents. He passed the money to Kingston, but he didn't bother to count it. "What, you ain't gone count it?" he asked with a finger pointed at the money, having seen him slid it into the pocket of his jeans.

"Nah, I'm not finna count this shit. Like I said, we have the same exchange every month. You know what chu suppose to bring to the table and so do I." he told him, staring him dead in his face. "I trust that you won't short me 'cause you don't wanna fuck up this arrangement. I mean, this is a good thing we got going here. You break me off my bread and I give you yo' drugs…the same drugs that allow you to compete among some of the best athletes in the NBA…without 'em, your good, but with 'em, your one of the best in the game."

"True, true, true," Tyjuan nodded his head. He agreed with everything Kingston was hitting him with. There wasn't any way he was going to fuck up their business. He needed the steroid the streets dubbed, Hercules. It was the best performance drug to hit the black market. It enhanced all of your senses and your strength. The only side effect was that its long term use could cause a heart attack, stroke and/or muscle deterioration. Still, that didn't stop some of the top performing ball players in the game from taking the drug. And why would they? Hercules had them playing like they were Gods on the basketball court.

"Besides," Kingston continued, his face turning into a scowl. "You fuck me outta mine, it ain't gone be The Boys with them badges that's coming to see you. Nahhhh," he shut his eyelids briefly and shook his head. He then pulled out a .9mm automatic handgun. As soon as Tyjuan saw it he stiffened like an erect dick. "It's gone be me and this pretty mothafucka right here that's gone be on that ass. You feel me?" he grabbed the back of his neck and massaged roughly as he stared him in his eyes, still gripping his gun.

"Y—yeah, I feel you. I'd neva cross you. You know me betta than that. We go way back to middle school, dawg." He claimed, looking scared as a bitch. He kept his fearful eyes on the gun in Kingston's hand and swallowed the lump of nervousness in his throat.

"I know. And I really hope you wouldn't cross me. I really do," he continued to stare into Tyjuan's face and massage his neck. "'Cause I'd hate to have to hunt chu down and peel yo' cap back. If I had to do that it would break my heart. And it would only break my heart 'cause I fucks with chu tough. I mean, real tough."

"Nah, nah, man," Tyjuan shook his head. "You ain't gotta worry about me. I'd neva do no foul shit like that to you, homie. I consider you a friend as well, and I fucks witchu the long way."

"Good." Kingston tucked his gun on his waistline and said, "So, I'll see you in a month, right?"

"Yeah," he nodded fast. "I'll see you four weeks."

"Cool. I got fifty stacks riding on this next game, dawg. Don't letta nigga down."

"I won't, especially now that I got this..." Tyjuan held up the bottle and smirked nervously.

"Alright now, have a good night." Kingston hopped out of the car and slammed the door shut behind him. He looked over both shoulders cautiously as he headed back to his car. In no time, he was sliding in behind the wheel and pulling off.

Once his plug was gone, Tyjuan sighed with relief. He then shut his eyelids and lay back against the headrest. He peeled his eyelids back open and held the bottle before his eyes. He smiled staring at the blue pills inside of the burnt orange bottle. With Hercules, he was what every kid wanted to be, all the bitches wanted to fuck him and he made enough paper to take care of his entire family. Without Hercules, he was just another poor black-ass nigga from the ghetto with hoop dreams.

Nah, fuck that! I gots ta be the man. I gots to, Tyjuan thought to himself.

"Me and you gone be like this," Tyjuan crossed his fingers as he stared at the bottle, talking to it, "Forever. You hear me? Forever." He kissed the bottle and stashed it inside of his hoodie. He then fired up his X5 and drove off, nodding his head to Future.

Tobe Chandler stood at the back of McDonalds, ducked off in the shaded area of the establishment. He was wearing a hood and basketball shorts. His arms were folded across his chest and he was impatiently tapping his signature sneaker. Occasionally, he'd glance at his watch and smack his lips seeing that the cat he was suppose to be meeting was nearly a half hour late.

"Fuck, man! Where is this nigga at?" He looked around and continued to tap his sneaker. Having grown frustrated, he pulled his cell phone out the pocket of his hoodie. Flipping the cellular open with his thumb, he opened his contacts and looked up the dude he was supposed to meet. Scrolling through the call log and finding the number he was looking for, he made to put the call in when he was blinded by bright headlights. He narrowed his eyelids and his head snapped around. He found a Honda Accord pulling up into the stall. It was close enough now for him to see someone's silhouette behind the wheel. Realizing that it was the dude he needed to see, Tobe shut his cellular and stashed it where he'd pulled it from. He watched as the driver's door opened and Kingston stepped out.

Kingston stood where he was for a minute as he held open the door and peered closely to make sure it was Tobe. Once his sight had registered who it was, he slammed the door shut and made his way over to Tobe.

"'Sup, my nigga? Forgive me for the tardiness. I know I'm late but I had some shit I hadda handle. You feel me?" Kingston asked as he slapped hands with Tobe and patted him on his back.

"My dude, you got me finna be late out this bitch. Now, I know you gone show me some love on the price."

"Fa sho, fa sho, I'ma show you some love." Kingston assured him. "I tell you what; shave five percent off the principle, how's that?"

"Now that's what I'm talkin' 'bout, good lookin' out." He slapped hands with him and embraced him. He then looked both ways and reached inside of his jean shorts pocket, which were hiding underneath his basketball shorts.

When Tobe pulled his hand back out of the shorts, Kingston saw him holding a fat ass knot of dead faces. After making sure no one was looking at him, Tobe went on to count up the dough he had to give to his plug for the drugs.
Once he was done, he passed Kingston the money and he slid it inside of his pocket. Right then, Kingston checked his surroundings as he reached inside of his jacket and pulled out a vial containing a neon blue liquid that appeared to glow. Tobe smiled like hell seeing the steroid known as Hercules in its liquid form. While the other ballers copped the steroid from Kingston in its pill form, he got his in the liquid form because he believed he got more bang for his buck. Kingston knew otherwise though. Still, he didn't give a fuck. Whatever floated his customer's boat was fine by him, just as long as he got paid.

Tobe stashed the vial inside of his pocket and looked to Kingston. "Yo', I brought my shit with me to shoot up, you mind givin' me a shot 'fore you leave, G?"

"Fuck no! I got other moves to make. You better have one of yo' flunkies hook you up. You a million dollar nigga, I'm sure you got plenty of 'em."

"Man, ain't none of them niggaz around, and I gotta get to the gym in a hot minute. Come on now, fam, please."

Tobe begged with his hands together, looking pitiful than a mothafucka.

Kingston took a breath and looked around to make sure no one was watching them. "Alright, buts let's do this shit in yo' car since yo' shit tinted out."

"Right this way." Tobe motioned for him to follow him to his Porsche truck. Once they got inside of the luxury vehicle, Kingston probed the baller's arm until he found a vein ripe for penetration. He then administered the shot and watched as the steroid worked its magic. Afterwards, he hopped out of the truck and made his way around it, heading for his vehicle.

Gotta start charging niggaz like that extra, wanting you to inject they drugs in 'em and shit. I ain't got no time for that. I'm out here tryna get to that bag, Kingston thought on his walk over to his vehicle.

Hopping into his car and slamming the door shut, Kingston pulled out the knot he made off of Tobe and started counting it. Seeing that the money was all there and accounted for, he folded it up and stuffed it into his pocket. He then fired up his ride and pulled out of the parking spot.

****

Kingston found a parking space at the end of the parking lot where there were very few cars. He brought his vehicle around and backed it into the space, killing the engine. He then activated his stash spot and retrieved three vials of Hercules. He stashed the drugs inside of his jacket and closed the spot. Next, he pulled out his gun and shut the glove-box. He looked through the windshield for the man he'd come there to see. When he didn't see any signs of him, he looked at digital clock on his cell phone. It was indeed the time he was suppose to meet him. As soon as he looked back up, an Expedition at the opposite end of the lot flashed its headlights twice, letting him know that it was the dude that he was waiting for.

With the signal given, Kingston stashed his gun on hip and hopped out. Shutting the driver side door, he adjusted his jacket and started in the direction of the enormous SUV. Once he reached the truck, its driver popped the locks and he slid into the front seat. He closed the door behind him and dapped homie up. His name was Donovan Sterling, and he was the quarter back of the Oakland Raiders. He was in Los Angeles vacationing with his wife when it occurred to him that he needed to re-up on Hercules. Well, not really. He actually had a closet full of the shit but it worked so good that he didn't want to ever run out of it when he needed it. And who could blame him? Hercules had made him the multi-millionaire he was today. So of course he'd want to have as much of the stuff around as possible.

"'Sup, my guy?" Donovan greeted his plug.

"Ain't shit, my nigga. Same ol' same ol', you know how I do. Another day another dollar, you feel me?" Kingston said.

"Most def', if it don't make dollars then it don't make sense." He nodded.

"Alright, as much as I'd like to keep shooting the shit witchu, I gots some places I need to be. So let's get down to business, shall we?" he reached inside of his jacket to retrieve the vials he'd gotten out of the secret compartment inside of his car.

"Fa sho'." Donovan rubbed his hands together in anticipation while smiling, excitedly. As soon as Kingston presented him with the vials the smile on his face spread even wider. He grabbed the vials out of his plug's palm and bounced them in his palm a little, testing their weight. Holding the vials in his hand right then made his arm itch. Although he'd already been juicing, it was something about a fresh batch of the shit that got him excited to shoot up again. "My man, always coming through for a nigga."

"No doubt," Kingston dapped him up. He was smiling too. This was because homeboy always spent good money with him.

Donovan activated the stash spot inside of his Expedition. He exchanged the money that was inside for the vials in his possession. Once he closed the stash spot, he passed the dough to Kingston.

"G' looking, my nig." Kingston stuffed the money into his pocket.

"Nah, good lookin' on yo' end, it's 'cause of you I got the nickname 'The Million Dollar Arm', you dig me?" he flexed his eighteen inch arms and kissed each of his biceps.

"That's mostly you, my nigga. You already have the talent, it's just my drugs that enhances it."

"However you wanna look at it, big dawg. Just as long as I stay as big as I am in the game, keep making these seven figures every couple of years, and fucking these fine-ass hoes, I'm willing to give thanks to whomever or whatever deserves it. You dig me?"

"Like a shovel." He dapped him up again and jumped out the truck. "Holla at me when you need that again, homie."

Donovan leaned forth and looked at Kingston through the passenger side window and said, "Oh, fa sho'. That goes without saying."

Kingston patted the roof of the Expedition and walked back to his car. Once he hopped in behind the wheel, he fired up his vehicle and moved to switch gears. Right then, his cellular chimed with a text message. He pulled his cell phone out and saw the name of the person that had sent it.

"Fuck he want?" Kingston's brows furrowed as he read the message that had been sent. Once he finished it, he hit the person back with a message and stashed his cell in his pocket. He then pulled out of his parking space and headed to his next destination.

CHAPTER FIVE

Eureka stepped out of the shower and snatched the towel off the rack. She dried herself off and wiped a circle in the fogged mirror. Staring at her reflection she was surprised she'd barely age. She still looked the same as she did when she was nineteen-years-old. She was forty-three-years-old now, and the only difference was her hair was styled in individual braids. She had slight crow's feet at the corners of her eyes and lines around her mouth that were barely visible. There was a little puffiness under his eyes and her hair was showing signs of gray, but this was due to her daughter being kidnapped, not her aging. If those turn of events hadn't occurred, Eureka wouldn't look a day over nineteen.

Eureka took care of her hygiene and left out of the bathroom, leaving the door open. The fog rolled across the bathroom floor and drifted out into the hallway, as she crossed the threshold. She entered her bedroom and started getting dressed for the night. Tristan was waiting for her in the living room. They were going to ride through the city posting up missing persons flyers of their daughter.

Eureka threw on her clothes and tucked her gun on her waistline, draping her shirt over it. She then put on her jacket and tied her braids up in a bun. She gave herself the once over in the mirror and headed out of her bedroom.

****

Eureka entered the living room to find Tristan at the fireplace looking at a portrait of their daughter, Cyan. She watched him for a while, before folding her arms across her chest and walking over to him. Feeling Eureka coming up behind him, Tristan glanced over his shoulder.

"Hey." Tristan greeted her and went back to staring at the portrait.

"Hey you," Eureka replied, staring at the portrait beside him.

"She's beautiful." He said of his daughter's stunning good looks.

"Yes she is. Our baby girl is the most beautiful young lady there ever was or ever will be."

There was silence as Cyan's parents stared at the portrait of her. Slowly, Eureka's eyes misted with tears and she turned away, whimpering. Seeing that his ex-wife was weeping, Tristan set the portrait back down on the mantle and turned to Eureka, hugging her. He rested his chin on the top of her head and rubbed her back, soothingly.

"I miss her, I miss her so, so much, Tristan. I want my baby back. I need my baby girl." Eureka sniffled and wiped her eyes with her hands.

"We'll find her…I promise. As God as my witness, I promise we will find our daughter." Tristan told Eureka as he held her at arm's length. "You hear me? We will find her. You believe me, right?"

Eureka sniffled and kept wiping her eyes, nodding. Tristan hugged her again and rubbed her back. He looked up at the ceiling and took a breath. There were tears in his eyes, but he batted them away. He knew he had to be strong for both their sakes. That's why he refused to show how vulnerable he was during Cyan's disappearance. He felt that if he allowed himself to fall apart then Eureka wouldn't be too far behind.

Tristan and Eureka's marriage had been on the rocks since Cyan's kidnapping. But it had gotten worse when Tristan turned to the bottle to cope with the tragedy. At first Eureka believed that his drinking would eventually subside, but she couldn't have been more wrong. Tristan winded up becoming an alcoholic. The poor bastard was a mess without his daughter, and the only way he knew how to deal with the situation was drinking himself into a stupor. Having grown tired of Tristan's self destructive behavior, Eureka gave him an ultimatum: seek help for his drinking or prepare for a divorce. Tristan denied he had a problem and kept drinking. And sure enough, Eureka made good on her claims and divorced him.

It wasn't until Tristan had a nearly fatal car accident while driving under the influence that he sought the help he desperately needed. Tristan eventually got himself clean and tried to reconcile with Eureka, but she wasn't interested in rekindling what they once shared. Losing the only woman he'd ever truly loved devastated Tristan, and he considered turning back to the bottle, but a part of him wouldn't allow him to succumb to his demons again.

Eureka broke Tristan's embrace and looked into his eyes. They held one another's gaze for a minute, and then they slowly moved in to kiss. Realizing what she was about to do, Eureka turned her head away. Tristan's brows furrowed wondering what caused her to turn down his advances.

"Have the telephones rung since you been out here?" Eureka asked Tristan as she walked towards the table which was filled with telephones. All of the telephones were black with red lights on them. The light would light up on whatever telephones that rung. There were four chairs at the table, two of which were pulled out. Lying on the seats of them were missing persons flyers with Cyan's face on them. There were also staple guns and tape to hang the flyers up with.

Tristan scratched his head confusingly about what had almost occurred between him and Eureka. Here he was thinking they were about to make out and then she threw a curve ball at him.

"Nah, none of the phones have rung since I've been out here."

"You sure?"

"Positive." He nodded. "I woulda heard it from where I was standin'."

Briiiiing! Briiiiiing!

The sudden ringing of one of the telephones drew Eureka's attention over her shoulder. She found one of the telephones in the front row ringing with its red light flashing. Quickly, Eureka raced over to the telephone and picked up the receiver. As she was placing it to her ear, Tristan was approaching from her rear. He listened closely as she talked to someone on the telephone.

"Yes, this is her mother, Eureka," She spoke into the telephone, with furrowed brows. "Yes, we still have the money. It's for any info or leads on her. Yes, I can meet with chu. Okay, lemme grab an ink pen." She looked to Tristan and signaled for him to give her an ink pen and something to write on. Tristan searched the table that the telephones were on and discovered an ink pen and a notepad. He handed it to Eureka and she hurriedly jotted down the information she was being given on the telephone. "Okay, I'll be there in a half hour. Thanks. Bye." She disconnected the call and finished writing the information down through her memory. Once she was done, she sat the ink pen down and tore the sheet of paper she'd written on from off the notepad.

"Who was that?" Tristan asked. His forehead was crinkled and his hands were stashed inside of his jacket.

"This guy. He says he has some info on Cyan's whereabouts. He says he wants to meet up, and to bring fifty thousand in cash."

"Fifty stacks? Wait a minute," he held up his hand and continued, "He wants fifty stacks to tell you some info on Cyan? How the hell do you know this isn't a setup or somethin'? For all you know this nigga could be lookin' to jack yo' ass for that paypa."

"I don't know," Eureka admitted. "But I do know I want my baby home, and I'm willing to do any and everything I have to in order to get her back safe and sound. So, if this guy has some information that can lead us to her, then I'll give 'em fifty G's for it. Hell, I'd give 'em a million if it means I'd get her back."

"Listen," Tristan began, placing his hands on either of her shoulders. He took a deep breath and continued, "I love and miss baby girl, too. It's just that, whoeva hit chu up has seen thousands of those missing persons flyas we posted up around the city. And let's not forget the magazines, news paper and commercial ads we took out letting people know that Cyan's missing. With all of that advertisin' people are gonna know we're loaded and we're desperate to find our daughter. Right now, we're lookin' like a meal ticket to the scandalous mothafuckaz that's out in them streets."

Eureka pulled away from him and said, "You think I don't know that? Me and my brotha are from the projects rememba? Our daddy was murdered and our motha was a goddamn dope fiend. We stole and hustled to survive. You know my story, or have you forgotten?"

"No. How could I?"

"Look, I don't know if this nigga is on the up and up about knowing where Cyan is, but there's a chance that he does. And that chance is a glimmer of hope for me, and right now, with the way I'm feeling, I need that hope. To be honest, if I was to find out that she was dead right now, I'd lose it. I'd fall to pieces. I lost my momma, my daddy…"

"Fear," He interjected, looking up into her eyes and waiting for her reaction. Although he was extremely gracious for the killa saving his son, Kingston's life, he was still jealous of the hold that he had on Eureka's heart. He didn't know what it was about him, but he could still tell that she was enchanted by him.

Eureka stared into his eyes for a moment and then she responded, "I'm not finna go there with you right now, Tristan. Right now, my only concern is Cyan."

Tristan nodded his understanding.

"Like I was saying, I lost a lot of loved ones. I can't take anotha loss; I'd wind up in a fucking straight jacket. As of right now, all I want to do is go see this guy and see what the fuck he's talking about. If he seems like he's trying to sell us some bullshit then we bounce on his ass."

"Nah, if this mothafucka tryna run game I'm puttin' hands on 'em, don't nobody play with this family, especially when it comes to a situation as serious as this one."

"However you want to play it, Tristan, but let's go see this guy."

"Alright." He nodded.

"Thank you." She touched his arm, affectionately. "Lemme go get this money so we can get on outta here."

"Okay." He watched her saunter off down the corridor to retrieve the money.

****

Tristan pulled around the back of the housing project that was still under construction. He killed the engine. He and Eureka jumped out of the SUV and tucked their handguns on their waistlines. Eureka came around the truck and stood beside her ex-husband. Standing together, with their hands inside of their coats and jackets, they looked around wondering when the man that had contacted them was going to arrive. Hearing a vehicle driving up at their rear, they looked to find a blue van coming around the unfinished tenement. The van parked on the opposite side of them and its driver hopped out. He was a stocky fellow who wore his hair in a Mohawk. He had ocean blue eyes and a small jagged scar that lead up from his top lip. He was dressed in an army green jacket with the Confederate flag on the back of it, a simple black T-shirt and worn brown leather boots. Thunderbolts were tattooed on either side of his head and his hands were inked as well. In fact, all of his ink claimed his affiliation to the Aryan Nation or his hatred for all non-whites. This piece of shit was a hatemonger and damn proud of it. His name was Remy.

"I take it you folks are Eureka and Tristan Teretto?" He stopped before them, looking between the two of them.

"I'm Eureka Jackson and he's Tristan Teretto."

"I'm sure he didn't need you to point that out."Tristan chimed in.

"I'm just setting the record straight." She responded, with her eyes on Remy as she spoke to Tristan.

"Divorced, huh?"

"Yep."

"Well, I'm sorry to hear that."

"Look, homie, I don't mean to come off rude, but let's cut the chit chat. We didn't come here to shoot the shit. We came here 'cause you claim to have some info on the whereabouts of our daughter."

"Yeah, I know where she is. I know exactly where she is, but I'm not giving you any info until I get that bag."

"Fuck that!" Tristan frowned. "You tell us where Cyan is and then you get the loot. For all I know you could dip off with that chedda."

"Fuck do you think you're talking to, you little fucking monkey?"

"I'm talkin' to yo' pasty white ass!" Tristan mad dogged him, looking him up and down like he wasn't shit. His trigger finger was itching but he didn't want to smoke his ass before he found out where his daughter was being held.

With lightening fast reflexes, Remy drew his handgun and pointed it at Tristan, occasionally pointing it at Eureka as well. "Shut up! Shut your fucking mouth, or I'll put a bullet right in it." He stared down Tristan and Eureka as he pointed his handgun between them. They stared him down defiantly. They both were strapped but he had them dead to rights. Any sudden move could prove to be fatal for them, so they stayed their hands. "Now, in case you haven't figured it out yet ladies and shit-heads, I don't have any information on your daughter. Nah, you see, when I saw this here flyer hanging up in my neck of the woods," he pulled out the missing person's flyer with Cyan's face on it from his jacket and showed it to Tristan and Eureka. "With a reward for $50,000 for any info leading to the whereabouts of this here baby chimp, I thought to myself, these niggerz are loaded. How loaded? I didn't know exactly, but their purse had to be pretty big if they're putting up five-hundred large for the safe return of their baby chimp."

"I knew it! I fuckin' knew it! I could fuckin' see it comin'!" Tristan spoke of the call being a setup to rob them of the bag they had up for any information on the safe return of Cyan. He mad dogged the racist-fuck and clenched his fists. His jaws throbbed and the veins in his hands bulged.

"Too bad you knowin' this was a setup didn't do jack shit for you, huh?" Remy snatched Eureka into him and turned her back to him, placing his gun to her head. When Tristan witnessed this, he went to draw his handgun. He'd almost pulled it from his waistline when another Nazis appeared behind him, as if by magic. His cherry blonde hair was pulled back into a ponytail and he had a scraggily beard which was tied off by a rubber band. He pressed his gun into the back of the Dominican's skull and relieved him of his handgun. Once he had secured the handgun at the front of his jeans, he placed his hand on his shoulder and continued to hold the gun at the back of his head. Tristan's body went rigid and he held his hands up in the air, palms showing.

"Nice and easy, homeboy, this here gun has a hairpin trigger. A slight tug will leave little pieces of your nigger brains all over the ground and this nice leather duster my girlfriend bought me for my birthday. Now, I know neither of us want that to happen, do we?"

"Fuck off!" Tristan spat heatedly.

"Is that the money in the bag?" Remy asked Eureka.

Yep..." Eureka replied heatedly, staring at him through the corners of her eyes. Her hands were held high in the air in surrender. She wanted to whip around and snap his neck badly, but she was at his mercy so she pushed that thought to the back of her mental.

"Cool." Remy looked to the raggedy blue van with the dents and scars on it. He whistled and the side door slid open. Two white dudes jumped down out of it. They had shaved heads and sported black T-shirts with the Confederate flag on them. One was toting a sawed off shotgun while the other had an M-16 assault rifle slung over his shoulder. They approached Eureka and the one with the sawed off snatched the bag from out of her hand.

"Jared, toss it over to Luke and let 'em count it up. Luke, make sure its fifty big ones there, okay?" Remy gave the orders like a military sergeant.

"I'm on it." Luke replied after he was tossed the bag. He walked it over to the van and pulled opened the passenger door. Sitting down on the seat, he unzipped the bag and began counting up the stacks of money concealed inside.

"You see? I told you this was probably gonna be a fuckin' setup." Tristan said to Eureka. "You let that tenda heart of yours walk us into a goddamn ambush."

"And I'd do it all over again if it meant a chance at us finding our daughter." Eureka shot back.

"You and yo' mattas of yo' fuckin' heart!"

"Fuck you!"

"Fuck you, bitch!"

All the Nazis looked around at one another in disbelief with furrowed brows wondering what the fuck was going on between Tristan and Eureka. They were going back and forth like they hated each other's guts or some shit.

"You wanna kick my ass? Well, come kick my ass!" Eureka bellowed at Tristan.

"I am, right now!"

"Well, come get some then!"

Swiftly, Eureka reached inside of her coat's pocket and pulled the trigger of her handgun. A bullet ripped through the pocket of her coat and entered the Remy's boot. The supremacist hollered out in pain and dropped his gun. Still holding her handgun inside of her pocket, Eureka brought it up and fired off another shot. Tristan moved his head out of the way of the incoming bullet just in time. The bullet went through the forehead of homeboy standing behind him and splattered his brain through the back of his skull. His eyeballs rolled to their whites and he was about to collapse. That was until Tristan wrapped his hands around the hand that he held his gun in. He placed his finger on top of the dead man's finger and pulled the trigger, back to back. Fire spat out of the gun and blew several holes in the shaved head Nazi's chest that was toting the sawed off. Having taken him out, Tristan turned the fury of his handgun on Remy. He opened fire on him until he collapsed dead.

Seeing homeboy that was counting up the money making a move on him, Tristan took the handgun into his hand and swung dude wearing the leather duster around. As soon as he brought his body around, he acted as a human shield and took the wave of bullets that was meant to take Tristan's life. Holding the already dead man up, Tristan outstretched his gun. Together, He and Eureka opened fire on the Nazi with the M-16 assault rifle. He danced on his feet as the front of his body was filled with black holes that ran with blood.

Just then, the headlights of a white van came on blinding Tristan and Eureka, temporarily. The vehicle sped forward and stopped short of the divorced couple. The van's sliding door opened and skinheads hopped out. They were all toting heavy weaponry. The driver's door of the vehicle was thrown open, but before the racist bastard behind the wheel could get out, two bullets came through the windshield, back to back. Blood splattered against the inside of the windshield as they projectiles hit their intended mark, directly in the forehead. The driver went slump where he was positioned behind the wheel, with his leg dangling out of the van.

A shocked Tristan and Eureka looked around for where the quiet bullet had been fired from, but they didn't find their sender. Before they knew it, smoke grenades were exploding at their feet. When they turned back around the skinheads were mad dogging them and lifting their guns. Seeing that they were about to open fire, Tristan and Eureka dove to the floor. At this time, the smoke quickly engulfed everything, leaving the Nazis narrowing their eyes and trying to look through the smoke to fire on Eureka and Tristan. The hate mongers swung their guns in every direction in anticipation of someone leaping through the smoke screen and attacking them. Little did they know, their ends would come from a far...via a sniper's bullets.

Choot! Choot! Choot! Choot! Choot! Choot!

The sniper's bullets ripped through the air fast and without warning, catching the skinheads' right between their eyes. The entre holes of the bullets were small but the exit wounds at the back of their skulls were large. Blood, brain fragments, and small pieces of skull went flying out of the back of the hateful white men's domes. They dropped right where they stood with their guns lying beside them.

Lying on their stomachs, Tristan and Eureka looked ahead at the skinheads lying on their backs with horror etched on their faces. Acknowledging that the sons of bitches were deceased, they looked over their shoulders, narrowing their eyelids to see through the smoke. Far off in the distance, they spotted a dark figure jumping from branch to branch of a tree. Once the figure had gotten close enough to the ground, he jumped down and landed on his bending knees, with the grace of a cat. When he stood tall, Tristan and Eureka noticed him adjust what they believed was a rifle slung over his back. He then made his way towards them, casually strolling and pulling something from his waistline. The closer he drew to them, the more of him became visible before the headlights of the Nazis van.

Tristan and Eureka slowly rose to their feet as the sniper approached. The only reason they hadn't started busting at his ass was because they figured he was on their side. If he hadn't been for their survival, then he would have surely executed them along with the skinheads.

The sniper had gotten close enough to Tristan and Eureka for them to see who he was, but unfortunately, he was wearing what appeared to be a wetsuit, neoprene mask and goggles. They took note of what he'd pulled out of his waistline also. It was a large caliber handgun with a muzzle attachment to silence the bullets it fired. The sniper walked right between Tristan and Eureka, like they weren't there, like they were fucking ghosts. He made his way over to two of the skinheads whose fingers were still twitching with life. Acknowledging their survival, the sniper finished them off with two well placed bullets to their hearts.

Having dusted off what was left of the racist men, the sniper tucked his handgun on his waistline as he admired his handiwork. Once he'd finished laying down the murders, he casually walked over to the driver's door of the van. Next, he placed two fingers to the pulse in the dead driver's neck to confirm his death. Satisfied, he turned off the headlights of the van and removed the key from its ignition. Having gotten the key, he threw it out over his shoulder and it landed in the dirt.

"Who are you?" Eureka asked as she stared at the sniper. Her brows were wrinkled with curiosity.

The sniper turned around to her and slid the goggles around his neck. He then pulled off the neoprene mask and revealed his identity.

"Fear?" Eureka's eyes grew big and she gasped, hand over her chest. "But I thought you were dead...Anton confirmed it for us."

"Look closer." The sniper responded.

Eureka blinked her eyelids repeatedly and peered at him.

"It—it really is you." Tears came to her eyes. She wanted to cry she was so happy to see him. It had been twenty-two long years since she'd seen or touched him, and she was aching like hell not to do so now.

As the sniper walked closer to Eureka, Tristan looked back and forth between them. He observed their interaction without saying a word. The sniper stopped before Eureka and she caressed the side of his face as tears slid down her cheeks. A slight smile curled both ends of her lips.

"It's Kingston, ma." The sniper told her.

"Oh, boy, you look more and more like your father each and every day."

"So, you've told me for the millionth time." He stared down at his mother as she continued to caress the side of his face.

"I know, son, I just can't get over the uncanny resemblance." She suddenly hugged him, taking him off guard. He wasn't expecting her to embrace him, but he welcomed it with open arms.

As his mother held him in her arms, Kingston looked over her shoulder at the man that had raised him like he was his biological child.

"Tristan," Kingston gave him a nod of acknowledgement and tapped his fist against his chest.

"Son," Tristan returned the gesture. This was the way they showed love to one another. They weren't big on that hugging shit. Besides, ever since Kingston found out that Tristan wasn't his biological father, their relationship had been different. The little nigga started showing him less respect and had even taken to calling him by his government name. Although Tristan chastised him about it, Kingston wouldn't budge. He refused to call him 'dad' knowing he didn't come from his nut sack. He would only address him as Tristan. This never changed, no matter how the boy was punished as a result of his defiance.

After a while, Tristan accepted the fact that Kingston was stubborn and things wouldn't change. He eventually got the boy to respect him like he once did before, but he'd have to grow use to him calling him by the name given to him at birth.

"How'd you know where we'd be?" Eureka asked her son, curiously.

Kingston pointed at Tristan and said, "Tristan texted…"

"I texted him our location," Tristan interjected. "My gut instinct told me that this meeting was going to be a setup, and I was right." he looked around at all of the dead bodies lying on the ground. There were bullet holes in them and horror was etched across their faces. "I figured it was best to have someone here to have our backs. You know what I'm sayin'?"

Eureka smiled and nodded at him, saying, "Smart man."

"Fuckin' genius," Tristan smirked and brushed imaginary lint from off his shoulders.

Hearing something in the distance brought Kingston's head around. He listened closely and heard police cars approaching.

"Well, I'd hate to be the one to break up this lil' family reunion, but The Boys are on the way and it's time we kick rocks." Kingston addressed his parents.

"I second that." Tristan ran over to the van and put the stacks of money back inside of the bag they'd brought along. Afterwards, he zipped the duffle bag up and motion for his family to follow him out of there.

Tristan and Eureka jumped into their car, watching Kingston pull off in his whip. When Tristan looked at Eureka she was on her cell phone. She had a concerned look on her face and was tapping her foot, impatiently. His forehead deepened with a line as he wondered who she was trying to contact.

"Who you callin'?" Tristan asked Eureka as he put on his safety belt.

"My bro," Eureka answered. "I've been blowing up his jack since we left the house."

"He hasn't answered you at all?" he asked concerned.

"Nah," she replied, pressing 'redial' on her cell phone. She listened as the line went straight to voicemail and blew hard, releasing a frustrated breath. "Ant, this Reka call me back as soon as possible, I'm worried about you. Love you, baby boy." She disconnected the call.

"Look, if you worried about Ant, we can always slide by that apartment he got over there on the Westside to see if he's there."

"Yeah, let's do that." Eureka said.

"I'm sure he's straight; try not to worry so much." Tristan told her. "He's probably just so high right now he doesn't know which way is up. Let alone where the telephone is."

"As bad as I don't want my brotha fucking with that shit, I really do hope that's all that's going on with him right now."

Eureka stared down at the screen of her cell phone. She was looking at a picture of her and Anton when they were much younger. Tears crept into her eyes and she bit down on her bottom lip.

Please, God, let him be okay.

CHAPTER SIX

"Antonnnnnn," Eureka called out to her baby brother as she beat on the door with her fist. "Open up, it's me, Reka."

Eureka waited a while but no one answered the door. She then pressed her ear against the door and listened closely for any sounds of movement or talking. When she hadn't gotten neither she took her ear away from the door and turned to Tristan. He could tell by the look on her face that she'd begun to worry.

"Eureka, I really don't think he's here, or he would have opened up the door by now." Tristan told her. They'd been standing outside of Anton's apartment unit knocking on the door, blowing up his apartment's telephone and his cell phone for the past thirty-five minutes.

"Something is up; I can feel it in my gut." Eureka motioned for Tristan to step aside. Once he did, she pulled out a couple of bobby-pins and jimmed the lock to Anton's unit. A moment later the front door clicked open. Rising to her feet, Eureka looked at Tristan and smiled. She placed the bobby-pins back in her hair and walked inside of the apartment. As soon as Eureka and Tristan entered Anton's place, she flipped on the light switch. They gave the modestly furnished unit the once over. The place was in complete disarray with dirty dishes and clothes strewn about. This didn't come as a surprise to Eureka being that Anton had never been a tidy person.

"Come on," Tristan nudged Eureka's arm as he turned towards the doorway. "If he's not here then he's most definitely in the streets. We can bend a couple of corners and see what's crackin'."

"Aye, what are y'all doing in there? I'm calling the authorities." A voice said from out in the corridor, startling Eureka and Tristan. The divorced couple's necks snapped to the doorway. At the end of their line of vision they found an elderly lady. She was standing in the doorway of the apartment across the hall. Her old ass was wearing a hairnet, glasses and flower decorated house coat. Her wrinkled hand held up a cordless telephone. She adjusted her glasses and began punching in a number. She'd managed to dial nine before a Glock was pointed at her. Tristan approached her hastily, scowling and holding a finger to his lips. The color drained from the elderly lady's face and she looked like she was going to have a heart attack.

Shhhh, hang it up." Tristan ordered the elderly lady and she obliged. She wore a face of devastation as she held a hand over her heart. Tristan snatched the cordless telephone from her, disconnected the call and dropped it to the floor. Using the heel of his sneaker, he stomped the cordless telephone until it came apart. He then looked back up into the elderly lady's eyes. He could tell by the expression on her face she thought he was the second coming of the Anti-Christ, and he wouldn't want it any other way. "Now, take your old-ass back inside of yo' apartment and watch *All My Children,* before the superintendant needs to put some fresh paint up inside of these halls." The elderly lady slithered back inside of her apartment and shut the door behind her.

Tristan tucked his handgun into the front of his jeans and turned to Eureka. "Let's bail. I know a couple of spots we can check for Ant."

Eureka shut the door behind her as she came out of Anton's apartment. She tucked her hands inside of the pockets of her coat and followed Tristan out of the apartment complex.

****

Eureka and Tristan emerged from the apartment complex in time to see a black Lincoln Town Car bend the corner, tires squealed as it turned recklessly on the avenue. The Lincoln skidded to a stop and its back door flew open. Moments later a man was thrown out into the middle of the street in front of Anton's apartment complex. The back door of the Lincoln slammed shut and it sped off down the street. Eureka and Tristan dashed over to the man that was thrown out into the street.

The man lay on his side groaning in pain. Tristan pulled the man over and his head fell to the side. Eureka's breath caught in her throat, she couldn't believe who it was. She was so choked up that she could barely utter his name. She swallowed hard and gave it a try.

"Anton," Eureka announced, feeling her eyes beginning to mist. Anton had taken one hell of a beating. His appearance was a testament to that. His face was bloody, lumped up and had what looked like twenty cuts covering it.

"Mothafuckaz!" Eureka bellowed angrily. In one fluid motion, she whipped her gun from her waistline. Gripping it with both hands, she closed an eye and took aim, hugging the trigger. Heat rocks spat in succession, murdering the back tail lights of the speeding Town Car. Once the vehicle had gotten so far that she could no longer engage it, she lowered her gun and looked ahead, nostrils flaring and chest heaving.

"Grab his other arm, we've gotta get 'em to a hospital." Tristan pulled Anton up and threw his arm over his shoulders. The youth's legs buckled so he grabbed him by the waist to keep him from falling.

"No, no, no," Anton shook his head, weakly. "I can't do it; I can't play the 'spital. I'm sick, man. I need to get right, take me upstairs. Lemme get a fix and I'll be okay."

Tristan looked to Eureka and she nodded, yes. She then threw Anton's other arm over her shoulders and moved to help him upstairs to his apartment.

****

Mobay lay back in the barber's chair with his eyelids shut as the barber lathered his baldhead and the lower half of his face, with shaving cream. As the barber was prepping him, his two bodyguards stood off to the side. One was standing up looking at the television mounted on the wall, which had a basketball game playing on its screen. The other bodyguard was sitting in one of the barbers' chairs and looking over a newspaper. As he read over the black and white print, his lips twiddled a toothpick at the corner of his mouth. While all of this was going on, the only other barber on duty was sweeping the loose clumps of hair scattered on the shop's floor.

A stranger wearing a trench coat and a hood over his head pulled open the barber shop's door. As soon as the door was fully opened, two hulking pit bulls came charging in over the threshold. One of the pits was black and had a shiny coat. The other was white and had brown striped patches. The beasts were oversized and covered in muscles. They looked more like genetic mutations than regular dogs. They stormed the barber shop snarling and barking, foaming at their mouths. Their presence startled everyone inside of the establishment. The barber's sought refuge and Mobay jumped out of his chair, running away. His bodyguards backed up and drew their holstered guns.

Bap! Bap! Bap!

One of the bodyguards held his gun with both hands and squeezed off, rapidly. The dog zig zagged as it charged towards him, dodging the bullets that were meant to kill it. The animal leaped high into the air and the bodyguard lifted his gun, firing at it. Bullets ripped through the air, narrowly missing the angry hound. The pit came down hard upon the bodyguard. The man hit the floor and lost his gun. The gun spun around in circles as it slid across the floor.

The bodyguard tried to fight the beast off, but his efforts were futile. The enormous beast latched onto his neck and tore his throat out. Blackish red blood spilled everywhere, soiling the bodyguard's button-down and staining the floor. The bodyguard lay on his back, eyes bulged and gurgling blood. He lay there helplessly as the dog continued to thrash its head around wildly, whipping the dying man from left to right.

Bap! Bap!

The other bodyguard let off on the other pit bull, but the beast was too swift in his approach. Before he could get a third shot off he was being pounced upon, slamming hard onto the linoleum and bumping the back of his head. Wincing, he peeled his eyelids open in time to see the animal's powerful jaws unlocking. His jagged teeth dripped wet with saliva, before its mouth covered nearly all of his face. The poor bastard hollered aloud in agony. Right after, his flesh was being torn clean off his face leaving its bloody skeletal bone structure behind. Wide eyed, mouth open, he thrashed on the floor until the merciless hound latched onto his throat. With a grunt and a violent jerk, he snapped the bodyguard's neck, killing him instantly.

Whack! Snappp!

The last standing barber swung the broom down across the dog's back, breaking the lower half of it. The breakage turned the broom into a spear and angered the hound further. It whipped its big head around ready to tear the barber limb from limb. Still armed with the broom, the barber jumped back prepared to go on the defense. The pit lunged at him and he stabbed it in its right eye, causing the snarling beast to holler aloud in pain. It backed away from its attacker, whipping its head from left to right, and trying to shake the broom handle out of its eye.

Seeing he'd wounded the animal, the barber ran towards the door. He'd gotten halfway across the shop's floor before the other pit bull leaped upon him. He struggled to fight him off, but the heavier mammal over powered him. The barber stumbled around, bumping into shit and knocking stuff off the counter. It wasn't long before the barber fell to the linoleum and the pit took advantage of him. The beast tore out his throat, killing him almost instantly. Right after, the pit with the eye wound came charging forward. He latched onto the barber's hand and tugged on it violently, until he tore it free from his arm. There was blood and flesh all over the place.

A horrified Mobay whipped his head from left to right, seeing the carnage that had unfolded before his eyes. He slowly stepped backwards towards the shop's door. Eyes bulged, mouth open, he swallowed the lump of fear in his throat. Realizing it was best to flee with his life while he still could, Mobay snatched the smock from around his neck and high tailed it from out of the shop. The copper bell residing over the barber shop's door rang as Mobay burst out of it. The gangsta cleared the threshold, leaving the bell rocking back and forth.

THE DEVIL WEARS TIMBS VI

"Haa! Haa! Haa! Haa! Haa! Oh, shit! Oh, shit!" Mobay looked back and forth over his shoulder as he ran as fast as he could down the sidewalk. His chest rose and fell rapidly, and his face became shiny from perspiration. Seeing his car sitting parked at the curb rejuvenated his stamina and he ran slightly faster. He'd just reached the car when he'd gotten the surprise of his lifetime.

Ba-thoom!

The stranger, who'd let the hulking pit bulls inside of the barber shop, landed on his bending knees on top of the roof of the Lincoln Town Car, crushing its rooftop like an empty soda can. As he stood to his full potential, Mobay looked up at him. The older man's eyelids were stretched wide open and his mouth was hanging open. He swallowed the lump of nervousness in his throat and scowled. Instantly, he pulled out his revolver and pointed it up at him, pulling the trigger. Smoke roared out of the barrel. Its bullets deflected off of the stranger's body armor and sparks flew everywhere. Mobay continued to pull the trigger of the pistol until it clicked empty. Once the revolver was spent, he threw it up at the stranger. As the revolver deflected off the stranger, he pulled his huge ax from where it was sheathed on his back.

Swiftly, the stranger brought the ax around and took it into both hands. Bringing it above his head, he swung it downward and buried it halfway into Mobay's skull. The older man's pupils rolled to their whites and he became slack jawed. His body twitched weirdly, and blood coated his face like paint.

The stranger snatched the ax out of Mobay's skull and he instantly dropped to the sidewalk. His killa then wiped the blade of his ax on the sleeve of his trench coat and placed it back where he'd drawn it from. The stranger took the time to admire his handiwork. He then looked up and whistled for his hulking pit bulls. The sounds of their hurrying paws filled the night's air as they came running towards him, barking. They stopped before their master with blood dripping from their chins, splattering on the sidewalk. One of them spat an arm out on the ground. As soon as he did this, the stranger leaped down on the surface and approached his van. He opened its double steel doors and stood aside. He whistled for the beasts and motioned them forward with his hand. The dogs took off running and leaped inside of the back of the van. Their master shut the double doors behind them and made his way around to the driver side of the vehicle. Opening the door, he slid inside behind the wheel and slammed the door shut behind him. He cranked that big mothafucka up, looked into the side view mirror, seen that the coast was clear and then pulled off.

****

Anton was feeling very much relaxed having gotten his 'medication'. Eureka released the tourniquet from around his arm and pulled the syringe from out of his vein. She then capped it and tossed it into the garbage can.

Anton had picked up the needle a few nights after Cyan had been kidnapped. It was his only vice when it came to coping with his loss. He'd tried alcohol, weed and cocaine, but heroin was on a whole other playing field. There was nothing like it. The high it brought him was like no other. It took him to a new plateau. He believed he'd met his first love in middle school, but boy was he wrong. He didn't get acquainted with the love of his life until he courted Lady Heroin.

"Good looking out, sis, you've become an expert at this shit." Anton proclaimed as he shut his eyelids and a smile stretched across his lips. "You sure you weren't a dope fiend in your former life?"

Eureka smiled as she placed the items Anton used to shoot up with inside of a worn brown leather case.

"Nah, you don't get to be one of Giselle Jackson's kids without learning how to shoot heroin. Yeah, I got plenty of practice thanks to momma." She grinned as she zipped up the leather case and laid it upon the coffee table.

"Try adding that skill to your resume." Anton chuckled.

Eureka picked up a hot bowl of water and a washcloth. She dipped the washcloth into the bowl and wrung it out. She then leaned closer to Anton and went about the task of cleaning up the blood that had dried upon his face.

For as long as Eureka could remember she'd been taking care of Anton. She felt like she was more like his mother than his older sister. And truthfully, she was, ever since they were little she'd been looking after him. Giselle was too busy getting off Johns to support her habit to be any kind of mother to either of them. So, it was up to her to make sure they kept a roof over their heads and something hot to eat. It for damn sure wasn't easy, but Eureka took the bull by the horns. While most teenagers in her position would have buckled under such pressure, she took the responsibilities on without complaint.

"Easy, sis," Anton winced as the wash cloth met the cuts in his face.

"I got this." Eureka responded as she concentrated on the task.

"Alright, Ant, what's the knowledge?" Tristan asked from the doorway of the kitchen, where he was posted up with his arms folded across his chest.

Anton took a deep breath and gave Eureka and Tristan the rundown on everything that led up to that point. "Now, he saying I gotta drop a bag on 'em…fifty grand. I'm like, alright, but he got me fucked up though. Nigga smoked my homie and beat the brakes off me, now he gotta pay with interest. Five-Owe, the pope, the president, the nigga standing in line at the supermarket waiting to pay for his groceries, anybody can get it behind mine. Straight like that, you feel me?"

Eureka frowned up and stopped cleaning Anton's wounds, rising to her feet. She stared down at him.

"We're not handling it that way. We're gonna collect the money and give it to 'em." She told him how it was going to go down. "I don't want anyone else getting harmed or killed."

"What?" Anton's face twisted. He looked at his sister like he didn't know who the fuck she was. "You talking about giving this old buster-ass nigga money after he done killed my mothafucking homeboy? Over my dead body! You got me fucked up, Reka!"

Eureka tossed the washcloth into the bowl of water. She placed one hand on her hip and pointed her finger in Anton's face as she talked to him.

"First of all, watch how you talk to me! I'm not one of them lil' bitches you be fucking with!" Eureka chastised him like a ghetto black mother would her son. "Now, it's because of Ball that you ended up in this situation in the first place. If it wasn't for him I wouldn't need to drop a bag off in this Mobay guy's lap. I'm sorry you lost your friend, I really am. But I will not lose you, too."

"Whatever, Reka, I'm not tryna hear that shit, man." Anton waved her off and looked away.

An angry Eureka grabbed Anton by the lower half of his face roughly, causing his lips to pucker up.

"Listen here you, lil' hardheaded fucka," she began. "I raised you like I pushed you outta my womb. Clothed you, fed you, and made sure you kept a roof over your fucking head. I was your mother when our momma was too strung out on dope to be one to you her damn self, so for as long as I have breath in my body you will show me the proper respect. Now, I say you letting this shit between you and Mobay slide. Is that clear, lil' brotha?" she stared him right in his eyes.

Eureka and Anton matched one another's gaze. Although he was a grown-ass man, he still had his sister on a pedestal. He looked at her like she was his sister and his mother. He loved, respected and honored her, and for as bad as he wanted to go against the grain, he decided to fallback. He didn't want to anger her any further. Because no matter how nice he was with his hands, he couldn't see himself squabbling with his sister. If his parents were to see that they'd turn over in their graves.

"I said, do I make myself clear, lil' brotha?" Eureka asked again, keeping her eyes on him.

Anton took a breath and looked away. He then looked back at his sister and said, "Alright."

"I can't hear you."

"I said, alright."

"Good."

Eureka sighed with relief and took a deep breath. Her shoulders slumped and she pulled her brother closer, hugging him, affectionately. She held him in her arms for a while, staring over his shoulder, eyes glassy.

"I'm sorry. I really am sorry how I came at chu, baby boy. It's just that…mannn, if I were to lose you…dude, I'd…" she shut her eyelids briefly and tears jetted down her cheeks. Sniffling, she wiped her dripping eyes with her curled finger and hugged her brother tighter. "I don't even want to begin to think about how I'd take it if something were to ever happen to you. I love you, Anton." She kissed him behind his ear and hugged him slightly tighter than before.

"I know. I love you too, sis. You gotta stop talking crazy though." He hugged her tighter. "Ain't nothing gone happen to me, you or that Dominican-fuck behind you." He glanced up at Tristan smirking. Tristan smirked and gave him the middle finger. "After Ball's funeral we gone hit these streets hard and find baby girl, you hear me? We gone find my mothafucking niece. That's on daddy's grave. You got my word on that shit." He told her as he held her at arm's length, looking into her tear streaked face.

This time Anton hugged his sister. They stood there wrapped in one another's arms for a while, before he decided to break their embrace. She wiped her eyes with the back of her hand and took the time to gather her wits.

"Look, me and Tristan are gonna go pick up this money and drop it off to Mobay. Lemme get the address before we go."

"Okay." Anton left the living room and returned with an ink pen and a piece of paper. He jotted down the address Mobay had given him and passed it to Eureka.

Holding it in one hand, Eureka looked it over to memorize it. Afterwards, she folded the piece of paper up and stuck it inside of her pocket. "Alright, I'm gonna get outta here. We'll be back before you know it."

"Alright." Anton replied.

Eureka hugged her brother again and kissed him goodbye. Anton and Tristan dapped each other up.

"Take care of my sister, man." Anton called out to Tristan as he held open the front door for Eureka to walk through it.

Tristan grinned and said, "I got this."

The door clicked as Tristan pulled it shut behind him and Eureka.

"Sorry, sis, but I can't let this one slide. Ball was my brother." Anton claimed, with determination on his face. His eyes bled seriousness and his heart pumped vengeance. Standing in the middle of the living room, he clenched his fists tightly. The images of what had happened to Ball flashed in his mind over and over again. It pained him to his heart to see his friend's death in his head, but he promised himself that he wouldn't rest until he avenged him.

I'ma get them niggaz for you, Ball. That's on everything!

Anton didn't waste any time getting ready for the attack he planned to launch on Mobay's ass. The nigga had tortured and murdered his homeboy and he wasn't about to let that shit slide. Anton may have been in bad shape, but he wasn't going to let up off of Mobay until his ass was dead.

Anton walked over to the furthest wall inside of the living room. He placed his ear against it and knocked on it, until he heard a hollow space. Once he did, he knocked on the wall in a specific pattern. Right after, the wall flipped over. On the opposite side of the wall there were an assortment of guns, knives, explosives and other weapons.

Anton buckled his ninja star belt around his waist. He then slipped a gun holster over his shoulders. He took a handgun from off the wall and ejected its magazine. He retrieved a box of ammo and begun loading bullets into the magazine. Hearing the telephone ring, he sat the gun and the magazine down on the living room table and walked across the room. He picked up the cordless telephone and answered the incoming call.

"Watts up?" Anton said into the telephone.

"Watts up, unc?" Kingston spoke from the opposite end of the telephone.

"Ain't shit, nephew. 'Bouta make this move right quick." He walked back over to the table where he'd sat the handgun and the magazine down.

"Who we got problems with? You need me to roll witchu, unc?" he questioned with concern.

"Nah, you good, I got this, nephew." He told him as he finished loading the bullets into the magazine of his handgun.

"You sure? You know it ain't nothin' for a nigga to pull up."

"Yeah, I know. I appreciate it, too." He smacked the magazine into the bottom of his handgun and chambered a hollow tip round into its head.

"No doubt," Kingston responded. "We family. If a nigga gotta problem with one of us then he's gotta problem with all of us."

"Sho' you right." Anton replied. He went to holster his gun and the lights in his apartment went out. Confused, Anton looked around wondering what the fuck had happened. Just then, his front door rattled from a powerful impact. Something or someone had attacked it with brute force. The sound was so loud that the unit slightly quaked.

"Yo', what the fuck was that?" Kingston inquired. He'd heard the loud noise that struck the apartment's door from over the telephone.

"I don't know. Hold on for a second." His forehead crinkled as he sat the cordless telephone down on the table top. He then gripped his gun with both hands and cautiously approached the front door. He'd gotten ten feet away from the door when it rattled again and again. Seeing what was happening, Anton lifted his gun and pointed it at the door. He angled his head slightly and waited for whoever was trying to break through the door.

Boom!

The upper half of the door went flying across the living room and splinters flew everywhere. The intruder that had kidnapped Cyan kicked out the remaining lower half of the door. As soon as he stepped his booted foot across the threshold into the unit, Anton opened up on his bitch-ass with a barrage of shots.

THE DEVIL WEARS TIMBS VI

Bloc! Bloc! Bloc! Bloc! Bloc!

The intruder did a little dance before he went crashing down to the floor. He lay on the floor still, seemingly dead. Anton, still gripping his gun with both hands, cautiously moved in on the man he'd dispatched. If he made the slightest move then he was going to put one in his brain. Anton had gotten close enough to spit on the intruder when his eyelids snapped open. The stranger threw a ninja star and it lodged into the barrel of Anton's handgun, locking it in place. He pulled the trigger and the weapon backfired, exploding in Anton's hand.

"Aaaaahh!" Anton screamed out in agony and cradled his hand. He staggered back from the front door, focusing on his ruined hand, wincing. When he looked back up the stranger was already on his ass. He grabbed Anton by the front of his shirt and threw him across the air.

"Unc! Unc! What's goin' on?" Kingston called out from the telephone which was still sitting on the table top.

Anton landed on his feet with the grace of a feline. Lifting up his shirt, he displayed the silver ninja stars that lined his belt. He snatched the stars from off his belt swiftly, one by one. His hand moved so fast that it could barely be seen as he threw ninja stars at the stranger that had broken into his home. Back to back, the projectiles went flying towards their target. The hooded man moved swiftly as he avoided the onslaught of lethal weapons. When the hooded man came back up from ducking the last of the stars thrown at him, he pulled his katana from where it was sheathed on his back. A gleam swept up the length of the curved sword and it twinkled at its tip. The man gripped the katana with both hands. He then nodded to the katana that resides over the fireplace, letting

Anton know he wanted him to get it so they could engage in battle.

Anton narrowed his eyelids into slits and his forehead creased, wondering why the stranger was willing to let him arm himself. Realizing he'd better take advantage of the situation, Anton darted over to the fireplace and snatched the katana free of its sheath. Standing where he was, he did fancy moves with the weapon, showing off his expertise skills. Throwing the katana over his back, Anton caught it and swept it across the floor in a circle. His head snapped up and he scowled at the hooded man, daring his ass to cross the boundary line he'd made. Without hesitance, the hooded stranger went charging at Anton.

Ching! Kiing! Bliiiing! Piiiiing!

Sparks flew in every direction as the men engaged in battle. They swung their swords at one another and a loud clash rung loud and angrily when they met. They took a step back from one another and engaged each other once again, trying to chop one another's heads off.

Ching! Kiing! Bliiiing! Piiiiing!

The men's swords clashed again, again and again. The fighting parties' shadows danced on the walls as the flames cooked the logs in the fireplace. Anton appeared to be holding his own, but he was exhausted and weakened from the wounds he received from Mobay's men. Still, he fought on bravely, dishing out his best moves, all of which his opponent deflected or took without much injury. While Anton was tiring, his opponent didn't seem to have even broken a sweat. Seeing this, drove him to push himself further…going harder.

Bwap! Wap! Thwop!

Gritting his teeth and arching his brows, Anton punched and back handed the stranger. He followed up by jumping up and kicking him in the face. The man's head snapped back and left his chin exposed. He stood frozen in this position. Anton's hardest blows didn't budge him. In fact, when he was attacking him, it felt like he was punching on a slab of concrete. After taking the kick square to the face, the stranger brought his head back down. Anton looked up at his opponent like he wasn't human. The man mad dogged him, with blood rolling out of the corner of his mouth. Keeping his evil eyes on Anton, he took the time to spit blood on the carpet

"Kill, maim, murder," the stranger said again and again. "Kill, maim, murder. Kill, maim, murder."

"What the fuck are you?" Anton stared up at the man. "Kill, maim, murder." The stranger repeated.

****

Having secured the bag they were supposed to drop off to Mobay so he'd leave Anton in one piece, Eureka and Tristan headed out to the location to meet the old gangsta. As soon as Eureka turned down the block of the barber shop, which was the meeting spot, she and Tristan's faces were lit by the red and blue lights of emergency vehicles. Wonderment crossed her and Tristan's faces. They exchanged glances and focused their attention back through the windshield. There was crime scene tape, police officers and homicide detectives standing outside of the barber shop. Bystanders stood on the sidelines watching as dead bodies were being rolled out of the establishment.

Eureka brought her car to a creep past the barber shop. The further she drove past the establishment, the further she and Tristan's turned their heads trying to get a look at what was going on. They were able to see blood splattered on the shop's floor along with those small yellow numbered tent fold things that are placed on the floor at murder scenes.

"Can you believe niggaz smashed Mobay and his bodyguards? Shit is crazy." Eureka and Tristan heard a young man sporting cornrows say to his homeboy, shaking his head. The young man and his homie were standing among the other bystanders watching everything unfold.

When Eureka and Tristan heard him say that they exchanged glances again. Having gotten the news that Mobay had been knocked off, Eureka focused her attention through the windshield and drove off.

"Guess we'll be holdin' on to that bag, huh?" Tristan asked.

"Yeah. The Lord works in mysterious ways; doesn't he?" she said, keeping her eyes on the windshield.

"You can say that shit again." Tristan replied as he took a pull from the cigarette he'd just sparked up. He then stared out of the passenger window, watching the streets and blowing smoke out of his mouth.

CHAPTER SEVEN

Anton gripped his katana with both hands. He went to swing his sword to decapitate his foe, but the man's gloved hand launched forward. It clutched him by the neck so hard that it caused his eyes to water and he gagged. Slowly, the man lifted off his feet and his legs dangled. Anton dropped his katana and grabbed the man by the hand he was clutching him with. He tried to pry his fingers from around his neck as he choked, but the son of a bitch had an iron-grip on him. Before he knew it, Anton was being flung across the room. He slammed into the wall, denting a hole in it and tilting a large antique mirror that was hanging nearby.

Before Anton could mount a defense he was being picked up again by his neck and flung across the room. Again, he slammed into the wall and made a dent in it. He landed on his hands and knees. Panting and dizzy, he looked up to see his foe strolling in his direction with his katana by his side. Anton's vision was blurry and he saw two images of the hooded man. That's when he bowed his head and squeezed his eyelids shut. Shaking his head, Anton looked back up and peeled his eyelids back open. He didn't see double anymore and his vision had returned to normal.

Looking ahead, Anton saw the katana he'd dropped while the stranger was clutching him at his neck, high off the floor. He knew he'd have to get his hands on it if he was going to stand a chance against him. Acknowledging this, Anton scrambled to his feet as fast as he could and charged forward. Nearing the katana, he dove to the carpet, tucking and rolling. Rolling in motion, he grabbed the sword and came up on his bending knee. Springing to his feet, he swung his sword upwards in an effort to chop off his opponent's head. The stranger ducked the swing of Anton's sword and thrust his katana, driving it through his torso. Anton's eyes bulged and his mouth quivered. He released his katana and it fell to the floor. Anton wanted to know who it was behind the mask so he snatched it out. As soon as he did confusion crossed his face. He couldn't believe the person staring back at him.

"Y—You—I thought you—you were—Arrrrrrr!" Anton squeezed his eyelids shut and threw his head back, screaming at the top of his lungs. His mouth was open so wide you could see all of the teeth in his mouth as well as his uvula. The stranger had lifted him high off the floor with his sword, causing him to slide further down his blade. The blood from Anton's wound expanded on his shirt and ran down the stranger's katana. The blade of the sword was now coated in blood and dripping on the carpet.

"Fuck you, fuck you in yo' mothafucking ass bitch!" Anton spat with hatred, staring down into his killa's merciless eyes. He harped up phlegm and spat a nasty bloody glob into the stranger's face. The man squeezed his eyelids shut and the bloody glob splattered in his face. He then peeled his eyelids back open. In his eyes, Anton didn't see anything. There wasn't any hatred, anger or remorse. His eyes were void of any emotion. He was indeed a killing machine.

"Kill, maim, murder. Kill, maim, murder." The stranger repeated over and over again. As Anton hung impaled on his katana, the intruder reached over his shoulder and drew his second katana. *Sniiikt!* He flipped the katana over in his gloved hand. Gripping it firmly, he drove it through Anton's lower abs. Fire ripped through Anton's lower half as he felt the sharpened steel penetrate his flesh. His eyeballs looked like they were about to leap out of their sockets and blood poured out of his mouth, dripping off his chin.

The intruder held his victim up in the air with his katanas. The blood from Anton's wounds slid down his killa's swords, over his knuckles and dripped off his wrists. For a minute the killa stared into Anton's eyes, watching the life slowly drain from them. Having seen enough, he snatched his swords from out of him and stepped back. As soon as he stepped back, Anton hit the floor hard with a thud. The intruder looked down at him, observing the blood from his wounds soak his shirt burgundy. When he looked back up, he was staring at his reflection in the crooked antique mirror hanging on the wall. Taking off guard by his hideously scarred face, he touched his face as if it was numb. He was horrified by what he saw staring back at him, but he shook off the unwanted emotion.

The intruder wiped one of his katanas off on his clothing and sheathed it where it was on his back. He searched the floor for his mask. Locating it, he picked it up and pulled it back over his face. Seeing Anton crawling towards something only his eyes could see, he switched hands with his sword and slowly strolled towards him to extinguish his life.

Breathing shakily, Anton crawled forth with his blood stained hands. His vision was blurring and he was growing faint from loss of blood, but he still kept crawling forward. Five feet away from him stood his smiling parents, Giselle and Bootsy Jackson, formally dressed in white from head to toe. A bright light surrounded them, making them appear heavenly. They stared down at Anton and outstretched their hands to receive him.

"Come on, son. It's time to go home." Bootsy said, his hand lingering in the air for Anton to grasp it. Anton's hand was inches away from taking his father's hand when his killa stood over him. He gripped his katana with both hands and aimed it downwards. His eyes were cast down on the area of Anton's body he planned to strike. Anton had just grabbed hold of his father's hand when the intruder brought his sword down. The deadly weapon went through Anton's back and broke through bone, stopping centimeters away from his heart. Anton's head and hand dropped to the carpeted floor, right after. The side of his face lay mashed against the floor. Seeing his body twitching, the stranger stomped the kilt of his katana. The weapon's blade impaled Anton's heart, killing him instantly.

Having finished off his prey, the stranger withdrew his katana from Anton's back. He flipped the sword over in his hand and sheathed it at his back where he'd drawn it from. He took one last look at Anton and took a deep breath which made his shoulders slump. Next, he walked towards the door, leaving the impressions of the bottoms of his boots in blood on the carpeted floor.

"Uncle Ant! Uncle Ant!" Kingston called out over the telephone, but he didn't receive an answer.

Lying not too far from the cordless telephone, on the floor, was Anton Jackson…dead.

****

Coming down the hallway on the 4th floor of Anton's apartment complex, Eureka and Tristan saw a crowd of tenants standing outside of his door. Their foreheads wrinkled wondering what had occurred. Thinking the worse, they went charging down the corridor. They pushed their way through the crowd of onlookers and found a bloody, dead Anton lying on the floor. Beneath him was a pool of his own blood which had dried and stained the carpet brown. His eyes were vacant and his lips were slightly parted.

Standing beside the couch was a tall geeky looking African American dude. He was wearing glasses and a plaid blue house coat. He talked to the 9-1-1 operator as he held the cordless telephone to his ear.

"Yes. Hurry, please..." the geeky looking dude disconnected the call. When he turned around and saw the pained look on Eureka and Tristan's faces, he froze in his tracks. Instantly, he knew that these were the loved ones of his next door neighbor.

"I'm sorry." The geeky looking dude expressed his condolences to Eureka, but she didn't acknowledge him. Seeing that she was lost in the scene before her eyes, the geeky looking dude decided to get out her way and joined the rest of the crowd in the doorway of the unit. He decided to go wait down stairs in front of the complex for the police to arrive.

Tristan stood behind Eureka crossing himself in the sign of the holy crucifix. His eyes brimmed with tears that eventually fled down his cheeks and dripped off his chin. He swallowed the lump of hurt in his throat, as he continued to look on at his ex-wife's slain younger brother.

"Damn, Ant," Tristan shook his head, hating to see Anton in his current state. "They did you bad, homie. Real bad...fuck!" more tears fled down his cheeks and he bowed his head, massaging his chin. His shoulders shuddered as he broke down sobbing. Hearing Eureka weeping, he looked up and wiped his eyes with the sleeve of his jacket. He saw that she was going to Anton and he attempted to stop her, but she shrugged him off. That's when he decided to let her be. This was her moment of grief and she needed to have it.

THE DEVIL WEARS TIMBS VI

Eureka sat down on the floor beside Anton, saying, "Oh, please, please, please, don't let this be happening."

The brims of Eureka' eyes turned red and her eyes pooled with tears. Wetness absorbed her cheeks and she sniffled. She pulled Anton over on his back and took stock of the damage done to him. The wounds inflicted by his killa's katanas left the lower half of him soaked in blood. So much blood had soiled Anton's clothing that it looked like he had gotten dressed in red from head to toe.

"Jesus, what did they do to you? What did they do to you, lil' brotha?" she asked with her hands pressed against the lower half of her face. She turned her head from left to right, taking in all of him. Suddenly, she squeezed her eyelids shut and took a deep breath, trying to calm herself down. "Okay, okay, this isn't real. This is a bad dream. All of this is a bad dream. I just gotta…" she made an ugly face and tears spilled down her cheeks. "I just gotta wake up, and everything will be back to normal." Shutting her eyelids, Eureka smacked herself harder and harder. She desperately tried to wake up from what she believed was a nightmare, but it wasn't working. When she opened her eyes again and looked around, she realized she was in the same place. And everything she was feeling and seeing was her reality…her brother was dead.

Eureka pulled Anton up into her arms. She held him and kissed the top of his head. It seemed as if the tears wouldn't stop cascading down her cheeks. She looked up at the ceiling, talking to the God Almighty, "Please, God. I'm begging you Father. I lost my father and my daughter. So, please, oh, please, don't take baby boy away from me. Please, don't take my brotha, God! I'll just die without him! I love him so much! We're all we've ever had; we've been through everything together. You've already taken so much from us, so much, but we managed, Lord. We managed…if we didn't have anything else in this world we had each other and a bond that couldn't be broken…" she bowed her head and squeezed her eyelids shut. She rocked back and forth with Anton's lifeless body in her arms. Her body trembled greatly and teardrops fell from her eyes, splashing on his bloody clothing. Finally, she looked back up, continuing her conversation with God. "And now—and now with his death—you're breaking that bond."

Just then, police car sirens wailed loudly, filling the air as they hastily approached. From their range of sound you could tell they would be pulling up any minute then.

The people crowding the door stared at Eureka as she grieved. They were all either crying or expressing their remorse through their facial expressions. Some of them crossed themselves in the sign of the holy crucifix. Just then, there was movement among the crowd as someone was trying to make their way through them. Once the crowd finally opened, Kingston emerged through the center of them. His eyes bulged and his mouth formed an O, seeing his dead uncle lying in his mother's arms. Instantly, his eyes pooled with tears and his entire form shook. He tried to say something, but he was too choked up. Seeing him breaking down, Tristan grabbed hold of him. He held the young man in his arms as he cried long and hard, tears soaking his cheeks.

Three hours later

Eureka didn't want to be home alone that night so Tristan offered to stay with her. When they came through the door the house was dark besides the light residing over the stove. Tristan flipped on the light switch and bathed the living room in light. He then peeled off his jacket and hung it. He told Eureka to head to the bathroom while he handled something. He recovered a black garbage bag and latex gloves. He then made his way to the bathroom where he found Eureka sitting on the lid of the commode. For a minute he stood in the door way watching her. Her head was bowed and her hands were dangling between her legs. She appeared to be in deep thought. She looked like she'd been through hell and back. And truthfully, she had. Eureka Jackson had ever reason there was in the book to have gone bat shit crazy by now, and winded up in a straight jacket at some insane asylum, but somehow she had managed to hold it all together. Tristan was amazed by her strength and perseverance. She was indeed a strong woman, probably the strongest woman he'd ever known.

"Come on, lil' lady, let's get chu cleaned up." Tristan said to Eureka. He switched hands with the black garbage bag and extended his hand to her. She took his hand and allowed him to pull her up to her feet. Kneeling down, he opened the bag as wide as he could and then stood back up. He assisted her in pulling off her blood stained clothing and placed it all inside of the garbage bag. He tied up the garbage bag and placed it by the door. Afterwards, he took her boots and set them aside.

Tristan turned the dials of the shower, adjusting the temperature of the water to his liking. He stuck his hand into the spraying water to make sure that it was perfect. He then thrashed his arm, dashing the excess water from his hand. Next, he outstretched his hand to Eureka and she took it. He helped her step inside of the tub and into the spray of the hot water. Eureka placed her hands on the wall and bowed her head, allowing the water to wash over her head and face. While she was doing this, Tristan was lathering her form with Dove body wash. He washed her up and then he washed her hair, thoroughly. When he was done, she told him to give her a minute alone. Once he had gone from the bathroom, Eureka allowed the water to wash over her body. She used the showers soothing liquid as mental therapy. It released the tension from her form, putting her a little at ease for the moment.

Suddenly, Eureka's mind was bombarded by images of Anton. She relived all of the happiest moments they shared. Within these happy moments she saw her brother and herself with their parents laughing, joking, playing, crying, praying over dinner, and spending time together like a family. At first she was smiling, but then that smile turned to trembling lips. A sadden expression crossed her face and tears slid down her cheeks. Pressing her hands against the tiled wall, Eureka bowed her head and broke down...hard. Her shoulders shook as she wept, tears dripping as quickly as she wiped them away. She hollered aloud and her pain streaked voice bounced off the walls of the bathroom.

"Oh, God, oh, God, why? Why, Lord? Tell me why?" Eureka's tears mixed in with the water that sprayed from the showerhead. At that moment, Tristan ran into the bathroom. He turned off the dials and took Eureka by her hand, helping her out of the tub one foot at a time. He snatched the towel off the rack, and when he turned around Eureka was throwing herself into him, wrapping her arms around his neck. He was stun at first, but seeing how emotional she was, he succumbed to embracing her.

"Shhhhh, everything is gonna be alright in time, Reka. I promise. It will be hard, but I'ma gonna be there when you need me. I got cho back." Tristan held his ex-wife in his arms and rubbed her back, affectionately. The wetness of her body soaked into his clothing, but he didn't pay it any mind. She needed him in this hour desperately, and he was going to be there for her. God himself couldn't keep him from Eureka's side. They may have no longer been married, but he still loved her as much as he did when they'd said their vows.

Dripping wet, Eureka cried and cried in Tristan's arms, until she couldn't cry any more. Once she was done, she looked up at Tristan with a tear soaked face and kissed him. Again, he was stun, and she could tell.

"I'm—I'm sorry. I didn't mean—" Eureka was cut short when Tristan tilted her chin upwards and kissed her lips, tenderly. He stuck his tongue inside of her mouth and they kissed, hungrily. They made 'Mmmmm' sounds as they stuck their tongues further into each other's mouths, kissing deep and passionately.

While they were making out, Eureka unbuckled Tristan's belt and unzipped his jeans. She pulled his boxer briefs down and grabbed his throbbing manhood. She stroked his thick veined dick up and down, causing pearly white pre-cum to ooze out of the head of it. Right after, she dropped down to her knees and licked him around the head of his dick, being sure to keep eye contact with him. She sucked him slowly and passionately, and then she built up speed. She had a rhythmic pattern and expertise as she worked his grown-man. The juices from her warm mouth slid down the shaft of his dick. She made humming noises as she sucked on him, taking more and more of him inside of her mouth.

"Ahhhh, shiiiiiit," Tristan threw his head back and shut his eyelids. He licked his lips in ecstasy and rose to the balls of his feet. Eureka's mouth felt amazing, so amazing that he never wanted to pull his dick out of it. "Ah, baby, baby, it feels so good. Oh, God, ahhhhh!" he looked down at her and she was stared right up at his ass, sucking his dick with a fierceness he'd never gotten from her in all of their years of being married. "Ah, yeah, suck that dick, suck that mothafucka!" he mad dogged her and clenched his jaws. He then pressed his hand at the back of her head and began humping her mouth. He started off slow, but then he sped up. The shit felt good to him. It felt real good! His dick grew harder, filling her mouth and causing her cheeks to swell. His powerful thrust caused tears to run down her cheeks.

"I'm 'bouta nut!" Tristan announced to Eureka. Instantly, she smacked his hand from the back of her head and took him out of her mouth. He looked at her ass like she crazy. "W—why you stop?"

"I don't want chu nutting yet. I wanna fill that dick between my walls." She looked him in the eyes thirstly as she stroked his dick.

"Fine by me." He slipped off his sneakers and kicked off jeans. Right after, he got down on knees and attempted to lift up Eureka's leg so that he could eat her pussy.

Seeing what he was about to do, Eureka stepped back from him. She then smacked him hard across the face, leaving his cheek stinging. He looked at her like *What the fuck is wrong with you?* She pulled him up to his feet. Grabbing him roughly by the lower half of his face and making his lips pucker up, she said, "What I just tell you, huh? I want some dick! I want chu to fuck me, and you better fuck me good!"

"Alright then, I'ma fuck this shit up out cho ass, too, lil' sassy ass mothafucka!" Tristan spat angrily as he pulled off his shirt and flung it across the bathroom. He then hoisted Eureka up and she wrapped her legs around his waist. Spinning her around, he walked her back towards the tub, kissing her on the way over. She grabbed hold of the shower pole on some Mimi, Love and Hip-hop type shit. As Eureka held firmly to the pole, Tristan sucked on her areolas hungrily and jacked his dick, making it slightly harder than it was before. A wincing Eureka looked down into his eyes as he pleasured her and himself at the same time. The sound of him beating his meat made her already wet pussy wetter. She couldn't wait to feel him deep inside of her hot gooey hole.

"Aahhhhh, fuuuck!" Eureka threw her head back as she squeezed her eyelids shut and clenched her jaws. She licked her lips seductively. She just loved when a nigga sucked on her titties. That shit drove her fucking insane. By this time, Eureka was humping Tristan and wanting him to fuck her in the worse way. "Mmmmm, I can't take it no more, baby. I want it. I need it." She shivered all over.

"You want what?" Tristan asked between sucking on the areola of her other tittie.

"You know what I want, baby, dont make me beg for it." Eureka said as she frowned up, licking her chops and biting down on her bottom lip.

"Yeah, I'ma make you beg, so start beggin' for this big mothafucka." He responded looking her directly in her eyes as he rubbed the head of his dick against her enlarged clitoris.

"Please, baby. Please, fuck me, I need the dick bad!" she begged like he'd asked, looking down at the swollen head of her ex-husband's dick. She watched as it teased her clit and caused her wetness to run down her thighs.

With his ego having been stroked, Tristan pushed himself inside of Eureka. The feeling of him entering her was a mixture of pain and pleasure. She hadn't been with anyone since they'd been divorced and that was two years ago, so she was tight as hell. Her walls felt like they were on fire, but once he started massaging her insides with his hardened dick, she found herself in the arms of ecstasy.

"Ahhhhh, yessss," Eureka said, as she held tight to the shower pole. She held eye contact with Tristan as he dug her out. Both of their faces were masked in sexual bliss and they couldn't get enough of one another.

"It's good, baby?" Tristan asked as he hoisted her legs further upon his waist and continued to hump away. His forehead and face were shiny from perspiration, and so was hers.

"Yesssss." She whimpered, with her cum oozing out of her and coating his manhood. He was hitting her G-spot and causing her walls to clench him. This caused more friction between them and she came some more.

Tristan and Eureka locked eyes. They held one another's stares as he pounded her out. The sounds of their dampened flesh smacking against one another resonated throughout the bathroom, bouncing off the walls. Their locking eyes while fucking turned them on. Her pussy got wetter, his dick got harder, his dick head swelled and so did her clitoris. They made the ugliest faces as the buildup in their lower regions became so great that they couldn't contain themselves. Finally, it happened!

"Unh! Unh! Unh!" Tristan threw his head back and gritted his teeth. He pumped in and out of Eureka, filling her pussy up with his cum.

"Oooooh, shiiiiit!" Eureka threw her head back and her eyes rolled to their whites. Her mouth stretched open as wide as it could as she hollered out in satisfaction. She experienced an intense orgasm and her entire body shook, uncontrollably.

She looked down to see herself squirting against the stubble of Tristan's mound. Tristan continued to stroke her pussy, causing her to squirt harder and faster. Her eyelids stretched wide open and her mouth hung open. She continued to shake while holding on to the pole. Suddenly, her body went limp, but Tristan continued to hump her front, oozing every last drop of his semen inside of her. His humping slowed and he found himself holding her, laying his head against her breasts.

Eureka allowed him to lie against her for a while, before she took her hands from around the pole. Holding her in his arms, Tristan walked her over to the center of the bathroom floor and laid her down. He laid his head back against her breasts as she stroked his hair and stared up at the ceiling. Tristan closed his eyelids and fell asleep. Eureka continued to stroke his hair, until she eventually closed her eyes and fell asleep as well.

Later that night

Eureka awoke on the bathroom floor with a sheet draped over her nakedness. She sat up where she was lying and looked around. Her forehead creased wondering where Tristan had gone. Looking up at the bathroom mirror, she found a note taped to it. Rising to her feet, she plucked the note from where it had been taped and unfolded it. She looked it over, reading it carefully.

What's up, Love?

Although tonight was wonderful, I'm not going to make it more than what it is. So, don't wet it. Anyway, if you need anything don't hesitate to hit me up. I'm one phone call away

Peace,

Trist

THE DEVIL WEARS TIMBS VI

Eureka folded up the note and sat it down on the porcelain sink. She then jumped into the tub and turned on the shower water. She took another shower and took care of her hygiene. Afterwards, she got dressed and dipped out to get the Plan-B pill from CVS.

CHAPTER EIGHT

Kingston sat on his couch taking pulls from a withering blunt as he stared at a portrait of him and his uncle Anton. In the framed photo Anton was training a young Kingston, holding up focus mitts for him to hit. Kingston was dressed in a black thermal and pants, attempting to attack the mitts.

Kingston's eyes were hooded from the O.G Kush he was inhaling. The whites of his eyes were red webbed and glassy. He found himself recalling his fondest memories of his uncle, and before he knew it tears were sliding down his cheeks. He didn't know who it was that had murdered his uncle, but he swore he'd get revenge.

I swear to God, Uncle Ant, the nigga that did that to you is done. Homie gone wish he never put his hands on my mothafuckin' family, real spit." Kingston wiped his eyes with the back of his hand and took another pull from his blunt. He blew out a cloud of smoke and took another look at the portrait. His eyes bulged and he dropped his blunt. In the glass of the portrait, he saw the same nigga that murdered Anton that night.

Kingston snatched his handgun from off the coffee table and jumped to his feet. He whipped around with his gun ready to fire. As he was about to pull the trigger, the intruder knocked the gun out of Kingston's hand with his katana. He then punched him in the chin and knocked him out cold.

****

Tristan sat on the couch eating a bowl of cereal and laughing his ass off at the cartoon playing on his "55 LG LED flat-screen. The blue illumination of the television flickered on him, as he cracked up with a mouthful of peanut butter Cap'n Crunch.

The doorbell's chiming garnered Tristan's attention for a moment. He glanced at the door but wasn't quick to get up to answer it. This was because the cartoons had his undivided attention. He sat the bowl of cereal down and wiped his mouth with the back of his hand, but kept his eyes glued on the screen. The doorbell continued to chime as he walked towards the door, keeping his eyes on the animated show. He was still looking back at the television's screen, when he went about the task of unchaining and unlocking the door. He'd just turned his head back around to the door, when he pulled it open. Before he could utter a word he was getting punched square in the face. The blow sent blood flying everywhere and him stumbling back in a hurry. Tristan bumped into the couch's arm and flipped over it, landing on the carpet. He looked up from the floor and saw a dark figure standing in the doorway. Blood was oozing out of Tristan's nostrils and the lower half of his face was crimson. He was seeing double through his eyes.

Tristan clenched his jaws and fists, eyebrows arching and nose wrinkling. He was pissed off that someone had the balls to show up at his crib and bust him dead in his shit. He'd scrambled to his feet when the intruder crossed the threshold and slammed the door shut behind him.

Tristan stumbled upon his feet and charged the intruder. Reaching him, he threw fists and kicks at him, with precision. His attacks came swift and without mercy, but the nigga that broke into his home ducked and dodged them with ease. The intruder ended up behind him, kicking him hard as shit in his back. The impact from the kick sent Tristan slamming up against the front door. As soon as he turned around from the door, the intruder rushed him, sending a flurry of punches to his torso. Each punch that was delivered caused the Dominican's eyelids to narrow and him to clench his jaws. While his body was getting pounded, Tristan reached out and snatched the ski-mask off of his attacker's face. His eyelids stretched wide open and his jaw dropped, seeing who it was that had broken into his home.

"You! What the fuck are you—oof!" Tristan was cut off by one hell of a gut punch that caused him to bend at the waist. His attacker grabbed him by the collar of his pajama shirt, whipped him around and pulled him into him. Still holding the collar of his shirt, the intruder gritted and continuously punched him in his kidneys. The pain that shot through Tristan's lower back caused him to throw his head back. He hollered aloud and displayed his bloody teeth. His eyelids were narrowed into slits and wrinkles were around the beginning of his nose.

When the intruder whipped Tristan back around, he tried ripping his heart out of his chest, but he poked him in his eyes. He howled in agony and staggered backwards, holding his gloved hands to his eyes. Tristan spat blood on the floor, seeing his reflection on the black marble surface, when he did it. Snapping his head back up, Tristan saw his opponent was at his mercy and decided to take advantage of it. In a snap of a finger, he charged him. Jumping up in the air, Tristan threw up both of his legs, slamming his feet into the hooded stranger's chest.

Having launched the attack, Tristan hit the surface and watched as the intruder stumble backwards hastily. Unable to catch his balance, the stranger crashed upon the coffee table, breaking it. The impact from the fall sent broken glass flying everywhere.

"Uhhh," Tristan grimaced, holding his side as he walked towards the stranger. Blood dripped from his nostrils and he was positive that two of his ribs were broken. Still, he was going to make this mothafucka pay for breaking into his shit.

When Tristan stepped to the man, he was still alive. The man's chest rose and fell with each breath he took. Tristan flipped over the couch cushion nearest to him, revealing a gold and black Desert Eagle. Keeping his eyes on homeboy, he picked the big gun up and went to point it at homeboy to finish him off.

"Unh!" Tristan grunted as his arm was kicked upwards by the intruder, as he pulled the trigger of the Desert Eagle. The gun fired up at the ceiling and debris fell in a trickle. When Tristan looked back to the intruder he was fleeing. Seeing him getting away, Tristan got down on one knee and aimed his gun at him. He shut his left eyelid and angled his head, pulling the trigger. He opened fire on the stranger as he ran around the living room. He continued to fire at him and missed, causing bullets to shatter and ruin furniture around the house.

The intruder made it inside of the kitchen and yanked open one of the drawers. As soon as he did, the silverware made a—cling—sound and one of the knives gleamed underneath the soft light of the kitchen. The intruder grabbed two steak knives and he looked up. Tristan was about to fire on him again, but he reacted before he could get off a shot. With fluid reflexes, the stranger started throwing the knives at him. Tristan moved his head from left to right, dodging the spinning knives flying at his face. Once the stranger had thrown the two knives, he kept snatched more from out of the drawe and started throwing them at Tristan.

Tristan moved swiftly as he avoided the spinning knives. Two more knives came at him. The first of the knives sliced Tristan on his cheek as he turned his head to avoid it. When he turned his head back around, he lifted his Desert Eagle and pointed it. He moved to pull the trigger and the last knife sunk into his forearm. Tristan threw his head back, squeezing his eyelids shut and screaming in agony. He dropped his gun and reached for the knife that was stuck in his arm. He yanked it out and it was bloody. He dropped the knife and looked ahead. His eyes bugged seeing the stranger flying across the room. He kicked Tristan flush in the chest. The impact from the kick slammed him into the flat-screen. The black glass cracked into a cobweb and electricity surged through the television. Tristan fell to the floor and the TV fell on top of him.

The stranger darted over to Tristan and threw the television from off him. He then grabbed him by his collar and lifted him off his feet, wincing. His head bobbled as he looked into his attacker's eyes.

"Is that all you got, cocksucka? I'm just gettin' started." Tristan harped up some phlegm and spit in his attacker's face. The glob of bloody goo splattered against the intruder's mask and dripped from off its brow. This infuriated the intruder and he slung Tristan like a rag doll. Tristan flew across the room and slammed into the far upper corner of the kitchen wall.

The force of Tristan's crashing into the wall rocked the kitchen and caused debris to fall to the floor. He hit the linoleum hard, grimacing. Dizzy and aching, he struggled to push himself up off the surface. The intruder ran into the kitchen and grabbed him by the back of his collar. He dog-walked him over to the metal subzero refrigerator and opened it. He then placed his head in the doorway of the refrigerator and slammed the door against it, violently. The intruder then yanked Tristan's head out of the refrigerator and slammed it against the side of it. Once he got tired of banging his head, he let him fall to the floor.

Tristan lay on the linoleum with a bloody and swollen face, rasping for breath. Looking up, he saw double, but remembered where he kept a chrome 12 gauge shotgun which was inside of his bedroom closet. Tristan started crawling towards his bedroom. He'd gotten about a foot away when the stranger lifted his boot and stomped his head. The assault busted Tristan skull and knocked him out, instantly.

The stranger stood over Tristan as he lay still. He then took a breath and walked off, leaving his defeated opponent behind. The masked man shut the door behind him as he left what he believed was a murder scene.

Thirty minutes later

"Uhhhhhh." Tristan moaned in pain and his eyelids peeled open. He slowly began to crawl out of the kitchen towards the telephone. Reaching the telephone, which was on the end table beside the couch, he knocked the end table over. The telephone landed in front of Tristan and he picked it up, dialing 9-1-1. As soon as the operator picked up, he told them as much as he could before passing out.

"Hello? Hello? Sir, are you still there? Hello?" the operator said as Tristan lay still on the floor.

****

Tristan lay in bed wearing a hospital issued gown. He was hooked up to a heart monitor and some other medical machinery to keep track of his vitals. His face, arms and parts of his body were swollen and bruised blackish purple. The fool that busted into his house had left him for dead, but a higher power decided to give him a second chance at life.

Eureka sat beside Tristan's bed. His hand lay in her hand as she caressed it, affectionately. Her eyes were pink and glassy. Her cheeks were shiny from crying and her nose was red. Occasionally, she'd wiped her eyes with a balled up Kleenex. Then she'd go back to caressing Tristan's hand, staring into his face and hoping he'd wake up soon.

Eureka had gotten a call from someone on the UCLA hospital staff informing her of Tristan's hospitalization. Instantly, she dropped what she was doing and shot straight up to the hospital. She tried hitting up Kingston, but he didn't answer. She started to worry but then she figured that he probably wanted to be left alone to deal with Anton's death.

"…what I'm trying to say is, we have been through a lot together. And although things didn't work out between us, I never stopped having love for you. You aren't just my child's father; you're my best friend." She took the time to sniffle and wipe her eyes before continuing, "I don't know who did this to you, Tristan, but I swear to God when I find them they're gonna pay for it. I swear on our child's life." She balled her hand into a fist, causing her knuckles to bulge.

At that moment Eureka's cellular vibrated and rang inside of her pocket. She pulled it out and looked at the screen. It wasn't a call she was getting, but a picture message. She looked at the message and saw Kingston gagged and bound. Below the picture there was a message. It told her where to come if she ever wanted to see her son alive again. There was also an address.

Eureka read the message aloud and said, "I'm coming, baby. Momma's coming to get chu, hold on."

Eureka put the cell phone back inside of her pocket and leaned over to Tristan. She told him what was going on with Anton and wished him a speedy recovery. Afterwards, she kissed him on the cheek and ran out into the hallway. Holding tight to her purse, she ran up the west wing of the hospital as fast as she could, her reflection showing on the waxed floor. When she made it past the nurse's station desk, a short muscular man in a duster stepped out into the hallway. This was Fear. He looked up and down the corridor, before following in the direction that Eureka had ran in.

****

Two armed military guards paced in front of the barbwire gates of the quarantined area. There were signs on the gates warning civilians not to enter or they'd probably get sick or be punished to the fullest extent of the law.

Hearing a noise at their left, the guards frowned and exchanged glances. One of them turned on their flashlights and shined its spotlight around, trying to see where the sound was occurring from.

Pewkt! Pewkt!

Suddenly, the guards were shot in the back of their neck by darts stained with sedatives. They winced and fell to floor knocked out cold. Eureka, dressed in ninja garb, jumped down from a nearby light post. She then made her way towards the guards she'd dispatched. She had a blanket in one hand and a hollow stick in her hand. She'd used the stick to fire the darts out of it. Eureka made her way into the street and confirmed that the guards were asleep. Pulling back her sleeve, she glanced at her watch to see how much time she'd have before they came to. Seeing that she'd have a little less than an hour, she went on to continue about her business.

Eureka dropped the hollow stick and took the blanket by both hands. She threw the blanket over the barbwire that lined the top of the gate. This was done so she wouldn't get snagged or pricked on her way over the gates. Once Eureka had done this, she scaled the gate and jumped over it. She landed on her bending knees, hands on the ground, looking around. Reaching inside of her garbs, she pulled out a pair of binoculars and looked through them. She saw Kingston gagged and tied to a stop-sign a few yards away. Two hulking pit bulls were circling him. The dogs were freakishly large and looked like they'd tear a nigga limb from limb. The menacing beasts appeared to be guarding Kingston, making sure no one could get to close to him.

Having spotted where her son was being held, Eureka searched the rest of the grounds through her binoculars. She was looking for homeboy that had called for her to meet him there, but she couldn't spot him anywhere.

"Where the fuck are you?" Eureka said to no one in particular. She then tucked the binoculars away and made her way towards Kingston, cautiously.

Eureka made her way up the deserted residential block stealthily. She made sure to keep an eye out for whoever had sent for her. Although she knew she was putting her life in danger by entertaining the meeting, she didn't give a fuck. She'd risk her life for any one of her children…she loved them both, immensely.

Eureka kept a watchful eye on the pits that were circling Kingston. She already knew how she was going to go about dispatching them. Her main concern was the whereabouts of homeboy that had called upon her. Without a shadow of a doubt she knew he was somewhere watching her that very moment, and she was at his mercy. Nonetheless, she was going to go follow through with her first mission, which was taking care of the hounds and freeing Kingston of his bondages.

Eureka pulled her silenced handgun from the recesses of her garbs. She held it with both hands as she made her way in her son's direction, hunched down. Seeing something gleam under the soft light of the light post, she looked down and saw she'd stepped into a metal net. Her eyes bulged and she mouthed 'Oh, shit'. In that instance, the net flew upwards and wrapped Eureka in it like a heap of fish being captured in the ocean. Her handgun slipped through one of the holes of the net and hit the sidewalk. She went zipping up the cord that held the net to the bulb of the light post.

"Aaaaahh!" Eureka's screamed aloud. The metal net began tightening around her and slicing into her clothing. The fabric of her ninja garbs started splitting and blood spilled from her cuts. Tears formed in her eyes from the pain. She clenched her jaws and reached for her ankle. She screamed louder and louder feeling the sharp net slice into her flesh. The blood from her cuts dripped to the sidewalk, splashing against it.

"Woof! Woof! Woof! Woof!" the hulking pit bulls barked and charged in her direction.

Looking up at his mother dangling from the light post helplessly, Kingston struggled to get loose from his bondages but he couldn't get himself free.

Snikt!

THE DEVIL WEARS TIMBS VI

Eureka pulled a knife from where it was sheathed on her ankle. The knife gleamed under the illumination of the light post. Its edges were outlined in diamond dust and could cut through almost anything. Tears running from the corners of her eyes, still clenching her jaws, Eureka sliced through the sharp metal cords that formed the net that held her captive. Instantly, she went hurling down to the sidewalk.

"Unh!" Eureka smacked down against the sidewalk hard, grimacing. She took stock of her damage and touched one of her wounds. When she did this, her finger tips came away bloody. Looking up, Eureka saw the pit bulls charging at her, with saliva dripping from the sharp canines in their mouths.

"Woof! Woof! Woof! Woof!" The hulking pit bulls were closing in on Eureka.

Eureka frantically searched the ground for the handgun she'd dropped when she'd gotten snatched up by the metal net. Recovering it, she took the gun into both of her hands and aimed it at one of the oncoming dogs. Taking a deep breath, and calming herself a little, she drew a bead on the targeted hound's head. The hound she was aiming at appeared to be moving in slow motion to Eureka. The only thing Eureka could hear was her heart beating, the barks of the dogs, and their paws hitting the sidewalk.

Eureka pulled the trigger of her handgun. The gun jerked and an empty shell casing flew out of the slot of it. A flame spat from the barrel of the weapon. A copper bullet came twisting and turning from out of the gun's chamber. The bullet ripped through the center of the dog's eyes and came out of the back of its skull. Brain fragments and blood sprayed out of the back of the animal's head. The hound fell to the sidewalk and his legs went straight up into the air. It was dead.

Having taken out one of the pit bulls, Eureka gave the last one her full attention. After she drew a bead on the beast, she pulled the trigger and sent a bullet through its forehead. Blood and brain fragments sprayed from the back of the creature's skull. The hound smacked down on the pavement, with its four legs going stiff, standing straight up.

Feeling something hard land and roll near her, Eureka looked to her right and saw a grenade. Gun in hand, she took off running. She'd gotten about six feet before the grenade exploded. The force from the explosion sent Eureka high into the air, flipping her forward. She landed upside down on the windshield of a parked station wagon, cracking the glass into a cobweb. She lay where she'd landed for a minute, wincing. Peeling her eyelids open and looking ahead, she saw a cloaked figure moving through the smoke and debris as it settled.

She witnessed whoever was wearing the cloak pull two katanas from their back.

Eureka peeled herself off the windshield and sat on the hood of the car, rubbing the lower half of her aching back. Jumping down onto the street, she looked around for her gun but she couldn't find it. That's when she realized she must have dropped it when she was lifted into the air from the explosion.

"Kill, maim, murder. Kill, maim, murder."

Eureka looked up. The cloaked man that had walked through the smoke and debris was standing before her. He went at her with both of the katanas, swinging the blades expertly. The swords made swooping sounds as they sliced through the air. The man in the hood tried desperately to take off Eureka's head, but she was too swift and agile to be beheaded.

Eureka ducked the swing of her opponent's swords. When she came back up she attacked him midsection with a flurry of punches. The impact of the punches slowly began to make the hooded man bend at the hip. Having brought him to eye level, Eureka jumped up and kicked him underneath his chin. The stranger went high up into the air, dislodging a grenade. The grenade deflected off a nearby parked car and tumbled out into the street. The stranger, still holding his katanas, flipped over in the air. He came down stabbing his swords into the street and sliding backwards. As he slid backwards, he dragged the blades and sparks flew on either side of him.

The stranger eventually stopped his sliding and stood erect. He flipped the twin blades over in his hands and went charging at Eureka. Wincing from the stinging of her opened wounds, Eureka slid into a martial arts fighting stance. She prepared herself to combat a foe who was significantly more powerful than her.

Seeing Kingston at the corner of her eye, Eureka looked to find him still struggling to get loose from his bondages. She gave him a look that let him know she'd free him from his restraints as soon as she took care of the katana welding stranger. Kingston nodded but still didn't stop trying to work the bondages from his wrists.

Hearing the hooded man charging at her, Eureka whipped her head back around. Her foe had his katanas held up like they were the antennas of a TV set. The lights from the light posts kissed off his blades and caused a gleam to sweep up the lengths of them.

"Kill, maim, murder! Kill, maim, murder!" the stranger repeated over and over again. His hateful eyes staring out of the holes of the ski-mask he was wearing. His jaws were locked and displaying his teeth. "Kill, maim, murder! Kill, maim, murder!"

"Oooh, shit!" Eureka's eyes bulged. She knew she was in a world of trouble now.

CHAPTER NINE

The stranger swung his katanas at Eureka again trying to make mince meat out of her. Again, she dodged his blades with little effort. She was fast, but apparently not fast enough. Her foe cracked her in the jaw with the kilt of one of his katanas. He then slammed the kilt of his other katana into the top of her skull, dazing her. She wobbled on her legs, and then he kicked her in the chest. Eureka fell backwards and pulled off his ski-mask. She hit the street hard, breathing heavily and clutching his mask. The hooded man's identity was revealed. Eureka was coming in and out of consciousness so she didn't quite see his face, but Kingston could see it clearly. He couldn't believe his eyes. He blinked his eyelids over and over again, believing his mind was playing tricks on him, but they weren't. It was indeed the person he saw standing before him.

"Kill, maim, murder! Kill, maim, murder!" the stranger kept saying over and over again. He then flipped his katanas over in his hands, holding them in a downward, stabbing position; he lifted them high above his head. He had every intention of stabbing Eureka through her chest. "Kill, maim, murder! Kill, maim, murder!"

Seeing his mother about to be killed, Kingston tried to holler something at the man aiming to finish her off, but the gag stopped his voice from escaping. Acknowledging this, he continued to struggle to get out of his bondages. His wrists were slowly begun to come loose, but he wasn't totally free from his restraints.

The shadow of the stranger holding his swords above his head shone on the streets, eclipsing Eureka. Seeing that she was about to be murdered, she figured she'd try to reason with the man before it was too late.

Eureka reached inside of her garbs and pulled out a photo, holding it up for the stranger to see. The man was in mid swing, bringing the katanas down towards her. He stopped midway once he saw the photo.

"Cyan, rememba?" Eureka called out to her only daughter. "Rememba me? Us? Your family?"

In the photo there was Eureka, Tristan, Cyan and Kingston. It was a family photo. Everyone in it appeared to be as happy as they had ever been.

The hatefulness left Cyan, the cloaked stranger's eyes, as she stared at the photo. She recalled the happiest times she had with her family. Each and every memory ripped through her mind. Right then, Cyan dropped the katanas and they hit the street, dancing at her boots. She then reached out to take the photo, but before she could take it a gunshot echoed throughout the night.

The side of Cyan's head exploded and she smacked down upon the pavement. Her eyes were stretched wide open and her mouth quivered.

"Useless fuckin' cunt!" Kingston spat furiously.

"Nooooo!" Eureka called out, seeing Cyan's head disintegrate and her body crash to the ground. Horror was etched across her face when they saw Kingston stand over Cyan and level his gun at her back.

"Boy, you can never find good fuckin' help these days, I tell ya." He spoke disappointedly and pulled the trigger of his gun.

Blowl! Blowl! Blowl! Blowl! Blowl!

Kingston put a few extra rounds into Cyan and tucked his smoking handgun on his waistline. Afterwards, he spat on the ground and observed his handiwork for a moment.

Tears came bursting through Eureka's eyes seeing her daughter lying dead in the streets. She made the ugliest face as wetness coated her cheeks. Her body shook uncontrollably. She looked up at Kingston with questioning eyes, wondering why he'd murdered his sister in cold blood.

Kingston brushed his shoulders off and said, "Niggaz, took my pops away so they had to pay...all of y'all mothafuckaz had to pay. Includin' you, ma. You was 'pose to have been his ride or die, but chu chose Tristan over him. Where the fuck was yo' loyalty?" he asked, looking her square in her eyes. Although his uncle Anton had killed Fear, his mother was just as guilty in his eyes, so her ass had to pay for his sin as well. He was on some 'fuck them all' type of shit. You couldn't tell the young nigga nothing, because he wasn't trying to hear it. "Y'all violated pops so I did what I had to do to make sure you paid for it."

"Where's my sister?" Kingston inquired.

"Over there, chained up." Homeboy pointed to the corner of the room. This was the same nigga that broke into the mansion and kidnapped Cyan. When Kingston looked in the direction that homeboy pointed in, he saw his sister, Cyan, chained up to a radiator at the far corner of the basement. She was lying on top of an old filthy piss stained mattress asleep. The sleeping gas she'd been sprayed with still had her out.

"Good. Y'all did y'all thang tonight." He dapped him up.

"Appreciate it, dawg. But that Hercules was the real star of the show tonight. I mean, I've always been nice with the hands, but that steroid you got made me a Super Me, you feeling me? I see why it's so hot in the streets."

"Well, I'ma kick you in a couple pills of the shit off the strength. You know, as a bonus."

"That's love." He rubbed his hands together and licked his lips, excitedly. With the help of Hercules he and his right-hand man were going to go on a robbing spree. Together, they'd rob everybody in the street life. As a matter of fact, he was going to see to it that they robbed Kingston's ass at some point and time. He had to get him. He knew his people were caked up, so kidnapping him for ransom was right up his alley, "Now, is that my purse?"

Kingston chuckled and said, "Yeah, this is you."

Kingston handed him the small Nike duffle bag. Homie took the duffle bag and sat it down on an old raggedy wooden table which had one leg shorter than the other. Dude unzipped the duffle bag and his eyes bulged with excitement. A smile spread across his face seeing all of the stacks of money in front of him. He took out a few stacks of dead presidents and kissed them, smiling harder than he was when he first saw the loot

"That's what I'm talking about, baby, that almighty dolla!" He took out another few stacks of money and kissed it, lovingly.

"You ain't gone call yo' man down here to count that up witchu?" Kingston said from somewhere behind the dude that was admiring all of the money he'd made for kidnapping Cyan.

"Nah, that's my brother. He trusts me. We gone count this shit up again once we touch the hood." He started stuffing the money back inside of the duffle bag.

"Wish you woulda brought 'em down witchu. I wanted to thank my nigga."

"It's cool, dawg. I'll tell 'em you appreciate 'em. Besides, if you toss in at least thirty of them pills, he'll really feel the appreciation, know what I'm saying?" he said, still putting stacks inside of the duffle bag.

"I got chu faded, big dawg. Don't even wet it."

"Y'all still in that same car or did y'all switch up?"

"Hell naw! We fried that bitch and got something else. We didn't need The Ones on us after that move we made." He told him as he zipped up the bag. "Got us a gold 2030 Ford Taurus."

"That's what's up."

Homeboy grabbed the strap of the duffle bag and slung it over his shoulder. He went to turn around, that's when a bullet went through his left eye and left a bloody, black gaping hole behind. Horror etched across his face and his mouth hung open. He dropped to the floor dead, with blood oozing out of his head. A scowling Kingston stepped to him, pointing his gun with the silencer on it at the back of his skull. He pulled the trigger, back to back. The gun slightly jumped as it spat fire at his limp victim. Kingston lowered his smoking gun just as the last empty shell casing hit the surface.

After the murder was done, Kingston took the bag from his victim and hid it behind a couple of boxes that were down inside of the basement. He then looked over to his sister who was still asleep. Next, he tucked the murder weapon on his waistline and headed up the stairs, throwing his hood on his head as he ascended the staircase.

****

Fleek sat behind the wheel of the Taurus nodding his head to the music pumping from the speakers. One of his arms hung out of the driver's window while the other held a withering blunt pinched between his fingers. Every so often, he'd take a pull from the blunt and blow out smoke. When he went to blow out smoke again, he met his red webbed, weed slanted eyes in the rearview mirror. That's when he saw Kingston walking up. This caused his forehead to wrinkle and he adjusted the rearview mirror, to try to see if he had overlooked his brother. He hadn't overlooked him. He wasn't there with Kingston.

"'Sup, my nigga? Where's, bro bro?" Fleek looked out of the driver side window as Kingston stopped outside of it

"Waiting for you in hell," Kingston's eyebrow arched and his nose scrunched up. He gripped his silenced gun with both hands and squeezed the trigger, rapidly. The deadly weapon spat fire at it Fleek mercilessly.

Choot! Choot! Choot!

Half of Fleek's dome exploded, sending brain fragments and pieces of his skull splattering on the windshield, dashboard and seats. Having laid homeboy to rest, Kingston lowered his gun and opened the driver's door. He killed the music and let the window up. All of the windows were tinted so he was confident no one would find Fleek's body before he was gone.

THE DEVIL WEARS TIMBS VI

Kingston shut the driver's door quietly and checked his surroundings. Realizing the scene was free of witnesses, he tucked his gun at the small of his back and walked off.

****

Kingston descended the staircase looking over at his sister. She was still asleep, which was good for him because it meant she wouldn't put up a fight. Once he removed the shackle from around her ankle, he hoisted her up in his arms and carried her up the staircase. Once he was outside, he stored her inside of the trunk and slammed it shut. He drove her down to 11th Avenue where there were several warehouses and factories that were out of business. He picked a warehouse that use to manufacture furniture. He parked around the back of the tenement and recovered Cyan from the trunk. Entering the building, he took her down inside of the basement. Down there, he had the place made up into a sleeping quarters. There was a twin bed, two buckets, two bowls for her to eat out of and an old box television set.

Kingston tied a blindfold around Cyan's eyes and put a gag-ball in her mouth. He then took out a hunting knife and carved up her face, badly. Cyan woke up from her sleep screaming and struggling to get out of her restraints. Seeing she was attempting to get away, Kingston straddled her and continued to mutilate her beautiful face. He sliced off her ear, and for good measure he hacked off her braids. Afterwards, he tore open her gown and sliced off her nipples. Once he'd done this, he dragged the tip of his knife up, down, and all around her torso. When he finished, the bloody wounds he left behind looked like bloody scribble scrabble on the poor girl's torso. Afterwards, he cut out her tongue so she wouldn't be able to speak again…to anyone.

THE DEVIL WEARS TIMBS VI

Kingston spent the next two months nursing Cyan back to health. Once her wounds had healed, he dressed her up in an orange jumpsuit, like the ones the county jail issued you. He made sure to keep her blindfolded at all times. He also made sure he talked to her through a voice changer device. He'd done it this way because he didn't want his sister to know who her jailer and abuser was.

Kingston fed Cyan and made sure she bathed every other day. He even made sure she had feminine products as well as other items for her hygiene.

Over the course of a year, Kingston would sneak down inside of the basement and beat the shit out of her while she was asleep. She'd eventually wake up out of her slumber and he'd knock her unconscious. He done this three times a night at different hours. This was done to drive her crazy and leave her mentally unstable.

Bwap! Crack! Wap!

Kingston fired on Cyan's face. He then cocked his leg back and kicked her in the mouth, breaking two of her front teeth and bloodying her grill. Her eyes rolled into the back of her head and she looked like she was about to pass out. Breathing heavily, he grabbed her by the back of the collar of her orange jumpsuit and dog walked her towards the iron chair he'd placed in front of the television set. Blood dripped from her bottom lip as she crawled forward on her hands and knees. The blue illumination of the TV screen shined on her face and caused her to wince.

Kingston snatched Cyan up and planted her into the chair. She was still a little daze from him going upside her head so she didn't put up a fight when he chained her to the chair. When the fog rolled back from her brain and her vision came back into focus, she looked ahead at the television screen. On the screen there were pictures of Eureka, Tristan and Anton. Then pictures of them alternated between footage of violence being done to people. There were bombings in other countries, drive-by shootings, stabbings, hangings, fights, people being maimed, etc. Then there was bold letters on the screen telling her to 'kill', 'maim' and 'murder'. These words would appear on the screen after pictures of Eureka, Tristan and Anton were shown.

Seeing this on the television, Cyan knew what her jailer was trying to do and she was going to try her best to fight it. She squeezed her eyelids shut and clenched her jaws. She bowed her head so she wouldn't have to watch what was on the television screen.

"Unh unh, open yo' eyes!" Kingston told her from behind his ski-mask, speaking to her through the voice changer device. When she wouldn't obey him, he grew angry and drew his gun. He then started smacking her upside the head with it. She still didn't open her eyes. Nah, she continued to fight off his command. Blood oozed out of her scalp and rolled over her eye, outlining her nose. Seeing Cyan wasn't going to open her eyes, Kingston put away his voice changer device and tucked his gun at the small of his back. Afterwards, he unsheathed a hunting knife from a brown leather holster on his hip and pulled her head back by her crop of hair. He then, one by one, began slicing off her eyelids.

"Gaaaaah! Aaaah!" Cyan screamed and hollered as her eyelids were being sliced off. Blood ran down into her eyes and over her cheeks. She tried whipping her head from side to side, but Kingston had her head locked in place.

Once he was done, Kingston cleaned her up and fed her pain killers. He then told her to watch the television or he *was going to kill her. Cyan still tried not to look at the TV, but when Kingston put his knife to her throat, and her blood trickled, she obliged him.*

"That's it. Good girl," Kingston said of Cyan obliging his command. He then ruffled her hair and walked back up the staircase.

Without any choice, Cyan was forced to watch the television or face certain death. The scenes on the TV screen shone on her pupils as she continued to watch. The images playing out in front of her were disturbing and caused her to cringe. She hated to see such bad things happen to people, and after a while she began to believe that her mother, father and uncle were to blame for the chaos she was watching.

"Eureka, Tristan and Anton are to blame for all that you see playing out before you on that very TV screen." Kingston's voice came over the intercom that he'd installed inside of the basement. "In fact, they are the ones that beat and mutilated your body. They deserve to die. They should be killed, maimed, murdered."

Kingston continued to comment on the footage as Cyan viewed it. He instigated the entire show and it fueled her hatred for those see saw on the screen.

"They don't love you. They never have. Look what they have done to you. They made you ugly, scarred you for life. You look like a freak now...a fucking monster."

Cyan's eyebrows arched and her jaws squared. She gripped the arms of the chair so tight that her knuckles bulged in her hands. Veins etched up her neck, temples and forehead. She was enraged and her eyes were glassy. Homegirl was seething. If she could have gotten out of her chair she would have drove her fist through the television's screen.

****

"Cyan! Cyan! Are you down here? I can't see. It's too dark." Kingston's voice rang out in the darkness.

"Uh! Uh! Uh! Uh!" Cyan responded the best way she could with her tongue having been carved out of her mouth. She sounded like someone that was mentally challenged.

"Hold on, I think I found a switch!" Kingston called out to her again as he pretended to feel around on the wall. Suddenly, the light came on inside of the basement and lit everything up. He found his sister lying on a mattress with her hands covering her eyes. She had spent so long in the darkness that the light felt like needles poking her pupils. She hollered out in pain and turned her head, trying her damndest to avoid the light.

Kingston made his way over to his sister. When he grabbed her hands and pulled them away from her face, she looked upon her big brother and saw that he was battered and bruised. His clothing was torn, he was missing a sneaker and his sock had blood stains on it. Once Cyan saw this her brows furrowed and she wondered what had happened to him. She touched the side of his face gently. Tears misted her eyes as she stared upon him in sorrow.

"Wha—whaaaaattttt—haaa—haappppennnn?" Cyan finally managed to get out as she looked upon her brother.

A teary eyed Kingston looked away and wiped his eyes with the back of his hand. Cyan cupped his face and turned him to face her. This time, she managed to ask him who had beaten him.

"Momma, daddy, Uncle Anton...they all beat me. They beat me and they did this to you." He pulled out a pocket sized mirror and held it before her eyes, showing her what she looked like. Cyan's eyelids stretched wide open and her mouth formed an O. she gasped at the hideous person she saw staring back at her and took the mirror from her brother's hands. Holding the mirror to her face, Cyan touched her face as she turned it from side to side. Tears welled up in her eyes and slid down her cheeks. She then opened her jumpsuit and looked at the ugly scars that were left behind as a result of her jailer's hunting knife. Instantly, she threw the mirror at the wall and it exploded, causing broken glass to rain down on the floor. Cyan broke down sobbing, and her brother comforted her as best he could. He kissed her on top of her head and rubbed her back, soothingl

"I managed to escape from the house. I overheard them say that they had you held prisoner down here so I came to bust you out. I beat up the nigga that had you held here and he ran away. I did manage to get the key though. Look," he produced a small silver key from out of his pocket and held it in the palm of his hand for her to see. He then went about the task of unlocking the shackle that bound her ankle

As soon as Kingston released the shackle from around his sister's ankle, Cyan rubbed the red bruise that had formed around her ankle due to the shackle being latched around it for so long. Kingston kneeled down and began massaging his sister's aching ankle. While he was doing this, she suddenly hugged him tight and kissed him on the cheek. She cried in his arms and he hushed her, telling her that everything was going to be okay.

"Save yo' tears, Cyan," Kingston lifted up his sister's chin and looked in her eyes. "The time for grieving over what has been done to us has passed. Now, we seek vengeance. Now we seek our pound of flesh. I don't know about you, but I want what's owed to us."

Staring up into Kingston's eyes, Cyan sniffled and nodded. Her face took on a serious expression. It was from this that Kingston knew that she'd agreed to go along with his plan of getting revenge.

"Good." He nodded. "I'm going to take you up to the cabins on top of the mountains, the same place where Uncle Ant took me to train. I will teach you any and everything you know about killing. Once you combine your training with this," he pulled out a vial of Hercules and she took it from his pinched fingers. She held it up before her eyes and studied its neon blue contents. "You'll be unstoppable. There won't be anything short of a God that can defeat you.

"Co—co—commmme on—let—let's goooo." Cyan stashed the vial inside of the pocket of her jumpsuit and took Kingston by the hand, leading him up the staircase and out of the basement.

Kingston took Cyan to the cabin on top of the mountains that his biological father, Fear, had trained his mother and her brother. It was there that he taught her how to kill, just like Anton had taught him growing up. Now Cyan knew how to fight thanks to the training she'd received from her family, but she wasn't as skilled when it came to the art of murder. That's where Kingston's expertise came in handy. He groomed her to be an emotionless killing machine. They stayed up in the mountains for six months straight, and by the time they came down Cyan was just as good of a hitta as any members of their family.

Kingston had Cyan on Hercules the entire time he was training her. She grew in strength and her body took on a muscular physique. She was covered in so much muscle that no one could tell whether she was a male or female, especially with her ski-mask on.

She had become just what Kingston wanted: a living, breathing, killing machine. One who's skill rivaled those of Anton, Eureka, Kingston and Tristan.

Cyan stood before Kingston in a ski-mask, hooded cloak and body armor. She was wearing the same costume that Anton donned when he was the assassin known as The Shadow. Her brother looked up at her like a proud father, happy at what he'd created in making her what she was that night. Stepping closer to her, he placed his hand on her shoulder.

"Tonight, we head into the city to claim our first drop of blood, Cyan." Kingston clenched his fist so tight that veins bulged in it. In response to him clenching his fist, Cyan gave him a nod. This was her way of letting her brother know that she was with him on his quest to revenge.

CHAPTER TEN

Cling! Cling! Cling! Cling!

The sounds of spurs resonated throughout the area, drawing Eureka and Kingston's attention. They strained their eyes looking through the darkness. The longer their eyes lingered the more the person wearing the spurs became visible. It wasn't long before they saw a short muscular man in a duster approaching from out of the dark. The end of his coat brushed over the ground as he moved forward, body swaying from left to right.

"P—pops?" Kingston leaned forward and took a closer look. He thought he was tripping, but obviously he wasn't. It was his father walking towards him. It was Fear.

"Fear?" Eureka's eyes bulged and her mouth hung open. She couldn't believe that it was her first love heading in her direction. "I thought—I thought you were dead. I thought Anton had left you to die."

"Nah, sweetheart, I'm alive and in the flesh." A scowling Fear said. Although he was speaking to Eureka, his eyes were focused on Kingston.

"Pops, you been alive all this time, man?" Kingston's forehead wrinkled.

Fear ignored his son and looked at Eureka, seeing that she was in bad shape on the account of him. He then looked to his son's sister, Cyan, who's head was blown off. He shook his head sadly, hating to see what had been done to her.

"What's the matter with you, son? You killed your uncle, your sister, hurt cho mother. What's gotten into you, youngsta?"

"This was all for you, pops, all for you." A smiling Kingston told Fear, looking around at the chaos he'd caused.

"You killed yo' uncle, man, yo' sister, too. Yo' own flesh and blood." Fear looked at him like there was something seriously wrong with him.

"Yeah, I popped 'em, but fuck 'em, pops! Fuck all of 'em, man." He said like it wasn't nothing, "Especially Anton, he's the one that left you to die inside of that fucking mansion," he pointed his gun at his chest and continued. "He left me a goddamn bastard, just like he was left; that jealous, vindictive cocksucka. He had it coming."

Fear looked away and shook his head, hating that the boy that came from his loins had grown up to become a monster. Having taken a deep breath, the ex-hit-man looked to his son with tears threatening to come out of his eyes. When Kingston saw his old man was on the verge of crying, he narrowed his eyelids and angled his head, looking at him as if he was an abstract painting of some short.

"Wait a minute, nigga, you got me confused now," Kingston frowned up and scratched his temple with his gun. "You actually crying over the mothafuckaz I wasted that didn't have any love for you? What part of the game is that? I avenged you, nigga. Excuse me, but I'm insulted, I thought cho ungrateful ass would be proud of me for doing all of this shit in your honor." he looked to his sister who he'd just murdered in cold blood. He then looked to his father. "You know, it's me that should be pissed at chu. I went through all of this fucking trouble, and yo' black ass wasn't even dead this entire time. What a fucking waste, man."

"What the fuck is wrong with chu, man?" Fear looked at his son like he was crazier than cat shit.

"What the fuck do you mean what's wrong with me, man? Ain't a goddamn thang wrong with me, fuck is wrong with chu?" his forehead creased with lines.

"You're a fucking psychopath , bruh! You fucking crazy."

"Don't call me crazy, man." Kingston's eyebrows arched and wrinkles formed across the beginning of his nose. "I hate that shit, I ain't crazy."

"Oh, yeah?" Fear took the time to wipe the tears from his eyes with his fingers; he then taunted his boy, "Coo, coo, coo, coo."

"Stop it! Stop it! Stop it!" he dropped the gun and smacked his hands over his ears. He wasn't trying to hear his father calling him crazy. It was something about being called *crazy* that really fucked up his head.

"Coo, coo, coo, coo, coo, coo." Fear slowly walked towards him and continuously taunted him as he advanced in his direction.

"I said, stop it!" the young nigga screamed on him, spittle flying from his lips. The veins at his temples bulged and looked like they were about ready to explode.

"Just what the fuck are you gonna do about it, lil' young ass nigga? You gone come kick my ass? Well, come get some, come get cho mothafucking ass kicked!" Fear snapped his wrist and a black twenty inch blade came from out of his fist. "Coo, coo, coo, coo, coo, coo, coo, coo, coo."

Fear's taunting was really getting to Kingston; he pressed his hands over his ears and screamed louder and louder on his father.

"Stop it, or I'll carve yo' goddamn heart out!" Kingston threatened his old man.

"All I hear is talk," Fear told him. "Coo, coo, coo, coo, coo, coo."

"Fuck you!" the young nigga snatched his gun up from the ground and came back up, blasting at Fear. Fear swung his fist up, down, and all around blocking the bullets meant to leave him on his back dead. Fear swung the blade so fast that its movements looked like blurs, and sparks flew from off the lengthy blade. Kingston continued to blast on his father until his gun clicked empty. Quickly, Kingston holstered his gun and snatched the machete from out of the sheath on his hip. Instantly, he went charging at his father, shouting a battle cry from his lips. He got about five feet away from Fear before he leaped into the air and swung his machete downwards.

Cliiiiiiiiiing!

The sharp metals clashed and sparks flew everywhere. Kingston came down on his bending knees and came back up, swinging his machete upwards. Sparks flew everywhere when the metals came into contact with each other again. From there, all hell broke loose as the father and son pair fought one another intensely.

Bwrap!

Fear swung his boot heel across Kingston's jaw and sent blood flying everywhere. The impact of the blow dislodged the machete from his hand and sent him flying across the air. He came down hard on the ground, rolling continuously until he stopped. Wincing, he picked his head up from the surface and spat slimy blood on the ground. He pressed his tongue against a tooth at the back of his mouth, which was loose and made him grimace painfully. He then reached inside of his mouth and jerked the loose tooth forward and backwards, causing it to become looser and looser.

Finally, he yanked it out of his mouth and spat more blood on the ground. Wiping his chin with the back of his hand, he looked at the tooth he'd pulled out of his mouth. Afterwards, he tossed it aside and spat some more blood on the surface. He reached inside of the small pocket of his cargo pants and pulled out two small blue pills, Hercules. He sat the pills on his tongue and closed his eyes as he swallowed them. Instantly, his heart started racing and he could hear it beating faster inside of his ears. The veins at his temples, neck and hands became more pronounced as his adrenaline pumped with a vengeance.

Right then, one by one, his muscles bulged. He peeled his eyelids open and his pupils were dilated. His hearing, sense of smell, strength, and sight were superhuman now. In fact, he saw everything in 3D, HD clarity. He was Kingston 2.0 now.

An evil smile spread across Kingston's face and he sprung to his feet as good as new. He stood even taller and bulkier than his father than he did before. His shadow left Fear in his shade, like he was some sort of big ass tree in the summer.

"I see, you couldn't see me with the hands, so you resorted to using some kinda fucking steroid, huh?" Fear looked his only son up and down, disgusted by him. "I thought I made the right choice leaving you behind for your mother and homeboy to raise but I was wrong. You grew up without me and it turned you into some weak, pathetic, emotional lil' bitch, with daddy issues. Punk-ass nigga," He mad dogged him and spat on his boot.

Kingston looked down at the nasty glob of spit on his boot and then back up into his father's eyes. His face twisted with hurt and hatred as he squared his jaws. The veins in his forehead bulged and he balled his hand into fists, causing the veins in them to become more pronounced. Before Fear could mount a defense, he was getting punched in the jaw. The blow connected with an impact that caused the bones of the ex-hit-man's jaw to crack. He went hurling backwards through the air, leaving one of his boots on the ground and losing his mechanical prosthetic.

The prosthetic clanked off the surface and Fear skipped off the ground like a rock being thrown across the surface of lake water. He skidded to a stop, lying still and twitching. His eyes were rolled to their whites and blood was running from his left nostril and mouth. He groaned in pain from the punch he'd received. In all of his years in the murder game he'd never been hit so hard. The punch his son rocked him with was the equivalent to being shot by a round from a shotgun.

"You're right, Daddy Dearest," Kingston began as he advanced in his injured father's direction. His pupils glowed neon blue and returned to normal. "Without the help of Hercules I wouldn't stand a chance against you. I've heard stories about you in the streets. Your hand to hand combat skills are legendary. There's never been any one that can match chu, not even uncle Anton. Let 'em tell it, and he did come close to beatin' you once, but a loss is a loss, no matter how close a mothafucka gets to victory."

"Uuhhh," Fear slowly began to stir awake. He sat up and rubbed his jaw, coming to the realization that it was indeed fractured. Staring ahead he saw two blurry images heading in his direction, a minute later the images combined and his sight cleared up. It was Kingston headed in his direction. He was walking casually towards him as if he didn't have a care in the world, and truthfully, he didn't.

"You see, the thing with me is, pops," He continued as he cracked the knuckles on both his hands, advancing in his father's direction, seeing him scramble to his feet. "I don't give a fuck about how I win, just as long as I win. It doesn't matter to me. I want what I want, and as of right now, I want chu at my feet bleeding and broken."

Once Fear was on his feet, he found that his legs were wobbly and his face was aching something awful. Still, as long as his limbs worked and he was breathing, he'd keep fighting until he couldn't fight anymore. Fear steadied his legs as best as he could and held up his fist. Well, his only fist, being that his other hand had been severed long ago. He tucked his chin to his chest and mad dogged his opponent as he approached.

"Although you share my blood, you're nothing like me, Kingston. Honor, loyalty and respect our things that I hold above everything else, even love." He swore to the younger version of himself. "I've gone against the best and won…by my goddamn self. I didn't need the assistance of anyone, especially not some kinda goddamn super steroid. So, even if you do kick my ass, when you lay down to go to sleep tonight, I want you to remember one thing."

"Oh, yeah? What's that, old man?" Kingston bent his neck from left to right, holding his shoulder and rotating his arm. He was stretching every part of him so he wouldn't pull a muscle beating his father's ass.

"You couldn't hack it when it came to bare knuckling it with the best, so you'll always live in my shadow…just like your uncle, but at least he had the balls to shoot me the fair one, man to man."

This statement enraged Kingston and his brows arched. His nose wrinkled and he clenched his jaws so tight that they pulsated.

"Shut the fuck up!" Kingston exploded with rage and leaped high into the air. Fear looked up at him as he soared high up. The young man came down, punching him at the top of his skull and landing on his bending knees. The skull-punch dazed Fear and left him at his son's mercy. The ex-hit-man swung and kicked at him weakly, missing him with every attack. Kingston laughed at him, manically. Seeing his chance to take advantage of Fear, he grabbed him by his neck with both hands and kneed him in his torso, rapidly. The back to back stomach blows caused Fear to wince. Once Kingston got tired on kneeing him, he held him by the collar of his duster and punched him over and over again. The repeated punches broke his nose and left the lower half of his face bloody.

"Like I said, I want chu at my feet bleeding…" Kingston hoisted his father high above his head in an attempt to break his spine. "And bro…"

Those last words died in Kingston's throat and he turned his head to the right. His right ear twitched as he heard something flying towards him at a sound that could never be detected by an Average Joe. Looking into the distance where he heard the sound coming from, he narrowed his eyelids and peered closely. In what was slow motion to him, he saw an assault rifle bullet hurling at him. At the last moment, Kingston pulled his father towards the bullet and it ripped through his thigh.

"Raaahhh!" Fear's eyelids stretched wide open and he screamed loud as hell. Blood ran from the gaping hole in his thigh and pelted the ground, as well as Kingston's boot.

For a moment things were silent.

Still holding Fear above his head, Kingston looked in every direction trying to find the sniper. Although it was dark out, he made out someone far in the distance pointing a rifle at him. As soon as he laid eyes on them a bullet was heading in his direction. Again, he brought his father into the way of the bullet.

"Aaaahhhh!" Fear screamed so loud that he nearly went hoarse, feeling fire rip through his calf muscle. Blood oozed out of his wound and slicked Kingston's hand wet.

"You—you mothafucking ghetto sniper, get cho ass out here now!" Kingston demanded, with spit leaping off his lips. When he saw that the sniper wasn't coming out from his hiding place, he brought Fear down to his bending legs and locked his powerful arms around his head and neck. The pressure he applied caused veins to form over Fear's face. Using his remaining hand, Fear tried to pry his son's arms free from his neck but his efforts were useless. "Come out now, nigga, or I swear 'fore God I'ma snap his bitch-ass neck!" With that having been said, Kingston watched as the sniper emerged from his hiding place and limped in his direction, still holding his rifle. The closer he got the more he filled out underneath the streets lights, until he was visible to Kingston.

The sniper pulled his hood from off his head and pulled the black bandana from off the lower half of his face. When he did this, Kingston could see all the cuts and bruises that he'd received from his brawl with Cyan. His wounds had slowly begun scabbing.

"Well, well, well, I'm surprised to see you here. I thought baby sis killed yo' ass, but clearly I've been mistaken." Kingston looked the sniper up and down, taking in his appearance, he said, "Excuse me for what I'm about to say. I mean, I mean no disrespect, but you look like shit."

"Suck my dick!" Tristan said and spat on the ground. He then looked to Fear and saw that he was in bad shape and losing blood fast. From the look in his eyes he could tell that he was feeling woozy and on the brink of fainting. "You okay, bruh?"

"Oh, yeah, I'm feeling just great." Fear said sarcastically and held up a thumb.

"Let 'em go." Tristan demanded.

"My nigga, you aren't in any position to be making demands and shit. I'm the one holding the upperhand and I say toss that puss' ass rifle to the ground. Do that, now!"

Tristan took a deep breath and reluctantly tossed his rifle to the ground. "The rest of yo' weapons too, nigga. What, you forgot chu raised me? I know how yo' old slick ass gets down."

"Right," Tristan went on to pull out the three guns that he had on him. They ranged from biggest to smallest. The last gun he pulled out was in a holster on his ankle. It was a black .22 with an ivory handle; he tossed it to the ground. Next, he pulled a couple of throwing knives from out of his sleeves and let them drop at his feet. Lastly but not least, he pulled out a grenade and dropped it to the asphalt. "That's it."

"I should fucking hope so," Kingston looked at the pile of weapons at his step father's feet. His eyes were as big as saucers when he saw everything he was packing on him. "Hell you do, rob the surplus?"

"Oh, my God, no! Not my baby, not my sweet, darlin', Cyan." Tristan broke down seeing Cyan lying on her stomach with the back of her skull blown out. Tears pooled in his eyes and obscured his vision. He felt weak in his knees and he buckled. He nearly fell, but he caught himself before he could meet the ground. "You killed her, you fuckin' killed her, you lil' black bastard, you! Aaaahhh!"

Tristan charged at his step son. Seeing his step father coming at him, Kingston threw Fear to the side and prepared to lock ass. As soon as Fear crashed to the ground, Tristan was on his step son like stink on shit. Even with his injuries he was moving lightening fast, throwing punches and kicks at him. The young man moved swiftly, avoiding the Dominican's attacks. He countered with a combination of punches of his own, wreaking havoc on the older man's body.

While the brawl was going on, Fear pulled the belt of his duster out and tied it tight around his thigh. He then pulled out his black leather belt and tied it around his calf. In doing this, he was hoping to slow the flow of blood so he wouldn't bleed to death. Afterwards, Fear looked to Eureka who was still lying unconscious on the ground. At that moment, the good times they shared whipped back and forth across his mind, causing a slight smile to grace his lips. The sound of fists pounding against flesh drew his attention back over his shoulder. When he looked, Fear saw Tristan leaned up against a parked vehicle getting the beating of his life from Kingston.

If I don't stop 'em, he's gonna wind up killing this dude, Fear thought to himself. He then picked up his mechanical hand and placed it back onto his stump. The prosthetic latched onto the placement on the stump. He then turned it and locked it into place, strapping it to his arm. Once Fear was done, he opened and closed the hand of the prosthetic to test its proficiency. Seeing that the hand was fully functional, he hopped back upon his feet. Fear then hobbled over to where Kingston was giving Tristan the beating of his life. Hopping upon the curb, Fear clobbered his son over the head which got him to stop beating on Tristan, instantly.

Kingston let a battered Tristan fall to the ground. He turned around to his father mad dogging him and squaring his jaws. He swung on his father, but he ducked it. Fear countered his boy by firing as hard as he could on his jaw, mouth and the side of his head. The blows from Fear's prosthetic hand seemed to slow Kingston down, but they didn't stop him. The brutish young man kept swinging on his old man trying to knock his ass out, but he couldn't manage to land a solid punch. Fear may have been older and wounded, but he was still quick on his feet.

"Eureka, Eureka..." Fear called out to the mother of his only son as he ducked Kingston's swinging fists. "Get—get Tristan and get the fuck outta here...now!"

Having heard Fear calling out to her, Eureka slowly came to and looked around. Seeing Kingston and Fear fighting she knew shit had gotten really real and she should follow his orders. So she got upon her feet as fast as she could and limped over to Tristan. She pulled him upon his feet and threw his arm over her shoulders. Together, they limped towards a white 2018 Dodge Charger. It was dusty and had dirt smudges on all of its windows. There were also cobwebs on all of its tires, but it looked like it was in working order.

Eureka leaned Tristan up against the trunk of the vehicle and ran around to the driver's door. Turning her head from the window, she slammed her elbow into the door's window, repeatedly. Slowly, the glass cracked into a cobweb until it eventually broke. Hurriedly, Eureka stuck her hand inside of the car and opened the driver's door. She then got on her knees and hotwired the car. As soon as the vehicle roared to life, she unlocked all of its doors and got Tristan. She helped him over to the front passenger seat and sat him down, buckling him in. After she slammed the passenger door shut, she looked up to see Fear fighting courageously with their son. Although she wanted to stop the brawl, she knew that there was little she could do, short of killing her own son. If she took his life she knew that there wasn't any way she could live with herself afterwards. In her heart, she believed that it was best to let his father handle him. She was confident that he'd make the right choice, like he always had when it came to them.

Bwap! Wop! Bwhack!

The last blow that Fear landed sent blood flying from Kingston's mouth. The killa followed up by kicking the deranged man in his crotch, causing him to double over and clutch his privates. As soon as he did this, Fear picked up the grenade that Tristan had tossed to the ground when he first came on the scene and shoved it inside of Kingston's mouth.

"I brought you into this world, son, and now I'm taking you out!" Fear roared and gave him an uppercut. The impact from his fist launched Kingston's head back. As soon as the young man hit the ground, Fear dove over a Cadillac Deville that was parked nearby. He hit the asphalt and Kingston's eyes bulged, realizing he had a grenade inside of his grill. He knew that his ass was about to explode into smithereens.

Blaaaaat!

Pieces of Kingston went flying in every direction. His bloody severed arms, hands and legs went high up into the air. His blood came raining down to the ground in droplets, splattering on the sidewalk. His spleen, chunks of his heart, pieces of his liver and brain fragments smacked down on the surface. The last thing to come back down was Kingston's head. It wasn't anything more than a bloody skull with little flesh clinging to it. The eye sockets, nose and mouth were hollow. The skull landed before Eureka's eyes in the street. Instantly, her eyes filled with tears and her bottom lip quivered. Her grief spilled down her cheeks and she broke down sobbing. Her teardrops fell from her eyes and splashed on the asphalt.

Tristan unbuckled himself and slowly got out of the Charger, wincing. He staggered over to his wife holding his side. He had tears in his eyes as well. He'd raised Kingston from a boy to a man. Although he'd tried to kill him, he still loved him like he'd come from his loins. The grief he felt didn't lessen knowing that the young man wanted him dead.

Tristan dropped down to his knees beside Eureka, just as she was picking up Kingston's skull and hugging it to her body. Her entire form shuddered and tears cascaded down her face. Tristan wrapped his arms around her and bowed his head. He cried alongside her. They didn't just lose a son that night, but a daughter as well.

Tristan and Eureka looked up at Cyan's dead face as she lay in the street. Her eyes were rolled to the back of her head and her mouth was wide open. At that moment, Fear came hobbling up beside Cyan. He removed his duster and draped it over her corpse, sparing her parents from seeing the horror etched on the poor girl's face any longer. Having just finished draping the trench coat over Cyan, Fear looked upon

THE DEVIL WEARS TIMBS VI

Eureka and Tristan. Although Tristan was still grieving, Eureka looked up at him with sorrowful eyes. Fear mouthed 'I'm sorry' and she nodded to him. This let him know that she understood his position in doing what he'd done and that she didn't have any hard feelings towards him.

Fear took in the pieces of Kingston that lay scattered over the streets. It saddened him to think that his son had died at his hands, but the way he saw it, it had to be done. If he hadn't went through with killing his child, then he would have taken out everyone, including his own mother.

At that moment, Fear eyes became glassy with grief. He took a breath and his shoulders slumped. Looking up at the sky, he shut his eyelids and mouthed a silent prayer. He then crossed himself in the sign of the holy crucifix. Once Fear finished his prayer to the Almighty, he brought his head back down. This time he was crying. He was crying just as hard as he was when his father had died from cancer. The tears came down his cheeks in buckets. He sniffled and wiped his face with the back of his hand. Looking off to the side, he discovered an old mop sticking lying in the alley. He hobbled over to the alley and picked up the mop stick. Picking up the mop stick, he used it as a cane and made his way over to Eureka and Tristan, limping. Slowly, he got down on his knees beside them and wrapped his arm around Eureka's shoulders. He cried and cried with both of her and Tristan. He cried for Anton, he cried for Cyan and he cried for Kingston. He cried for all of their loved ones that died.

CHAPTER ELEVEN

A week later

After Cyan, Anton and Kingston's funeral

Friends and family came out to the mansion once the funeral was over. They ate, laughed, talked and shared their fondest memories of their deceased loved ones. As the day went on, people slowly started to disperse, wishing Eureka, Tristan and Fear well before leaving the estate. After a while, the aforementioned were all that were left inside of the mansion.

Fear leaned on his cane as he looked over the family portraits occupying the mantle. There were portraits of Tristan, Eureka, Anton, Kingston and Cyan. There were also portraits up there of them as a family, but what stood out the most to him were Kingston's baby pictures. As soon as Fear laid eyes on them, a smile spread across his lips and he picked up one of the portraits. He was so close to the portrait he could see his reflection in the glass. He smiled even harder thinking of how much his boy resembled him.

Fear kissed the portrait. Bringing it back from his face, he saw a scowling Tristan in the reflection of the portrait's glass. A frown crossed Fear's face and then fire ripped through his back.

"Ahhhhh!" Fear squeezed his eyelids shut and hollered out. He dropped the portrait and it hit the floor, cracking its glass. Dropping his cane, he hunched over and reached for the wound in his back. Turning around, he found Tristan with a Berretta with a silencer on its barrel. Tristan squeezed the trigger of his gun again and fired ripped through Fear's stomach. The killa grabbed his torso and stumbled backwards in a hurry. He bumped into the mantle and the portraits fell to the floor in a chaotic clatter. All of the glass of the portraits cracked, just as Fear slid to the floor. He sat where he was holding his torso and looking down at his bullet wound. The lower half of his shirt was quickly being absorbed by his blood. He blinked his eyelids over and over again and clenched jaws. He did this to combat the pain that was wreaking havoc on him.

"I bet chu waitin' for Eureka to somehow swoop up in this bitch and save that ass, huh?" Tristan asked. He walked over to the mini bar, sat a glass upright and picked up a scooper. He shoveled some ice cubes into his glass. "Well, you can forget about that, homeboy. You see, wifey's takin' a long needed nap. That's right, I gave her lil' ass a sedative. I didn't wanna off her yet. Naahhh," he shook his head. "Not just yet. I'ma torture her somethin' awful before I seal her fate, you feelin' me, dawg?"

Tristan sat the scooper down and picked up a bottle of cognac. He removed the cork and poured the glass halfway full. He swirled the cubes around inside of the glass a little, and then he took a sip. Hissing, he allowed the liquor to settle in his belly. Next, he took another sip and turned his attention back to Fear.

"I know what chu thinkin', how could he kill her when he claimed to love her? I mean, she was my wife for Christ sake, right? Yeah, well, I hear ya, but blood is thicka than water." He sat the glass of alcohol down and lifted up his pants leg. On the side of his muscular hairy leg was a fading tattoo, *R.I. P Constance*. When Fear saw his old partner's name his eyelids stretched wide open. He tried to say something but blood spilled over his bottom lip. "Yeah, lil' mama was my family…my cousin. I did love Eureka. I mean, truly loved her. I loved her so much that I almost didn't follow Constance's wishes. She wanted me to kill you, Eureka and Anton."

The doorbell chimed. Tristan stopped chopping up the potatoes for his stew and sat his knife down on the chopping board. He then wiped his hands off on his apron and took a quick sip of red wine before sitting it down and heading for the door.

The doorbell chimed again.

"I'm comin', hold up." Tristan called out to whoever was ringing his doorbell. Having reached the front door, Tristan glanced through the peephole. His face balled up when he didn't see anyone standing on the other side of the door. He was about to go back to chopping up the potatoes for his stew, but his curiosity got the best of him.

Tristan unchained and unlocked the door. He pulled the door open and found a package at his feet. His brows creased wondering who had left the box on his porch. He ran out into his yard. Holding his hand above his brows, he looked up and down the street, but he didn't see anyone that could have left the package. It was a bright and sunny day. The only person out was the old Korean dude down the street, and he was mowing his lawn.

Tristan picked up the package. He shut the door behind him and locked it. Walking back towards the kitchen, he frowned and shook the box, wondering what was inside of it. He then placed his ear to the box to see if he would hear any ticking in it. This was his way of seeing if there was a ticking time-bomb inside of the box. Realizing there wasn't such a thing inside of the box, he shrugged and decided to open it.

"Fuck it." Tristan picked up the butcher's knife he'd placed on the chopping board and cut the tape off of the box. Sitting the knife aside, he opened the box and revealed what was inside. Inside of the box there were three photographs. There was one of a man, a young woman and a boy. This was Fear, Eureka and Anton. There was also a .9mm Beretta with a silencer attachment on its barrel and an envelope. He picked up the envelope and turned it over. On the opposite side of the envelope it read, Burn After Reading.

Tristan tore open the envelope and removed the folded letter inside. He unfolded the letter and read over it.

What's up, Cousin?

If you're reading this right now then I'm dead. Yeah, that's right. They killed my ass! I'm not tripping though, with all of the mothafuckas me and old boy took out of the game, I knew my time was bound to come...

Tristan's eyes misted with tears as he went on reading the letter. In the letter he found out some very pertinent information on Fear, Eureka and Anton. He was informed on their habits, places they frequented, things they liked and disliked and their personalities.

Avenge me, cousin. Do for me what I cannot do from my grave.

I love you,

Constance

Tears slid down Tristan's face as he balled up the letter and the envelope together. He walked it over to the stove and turned the dial on it, igniting the blue flames of the burner. Tristan dropped the balled up letter onto the burner, *watching the flames licked at it until it turned into black ashes. Afterwards, he walked back over to the counter and picked up the Berretta with the silencer attachment on its barrel.*

Tristan picked up the handgun and gripped it with both hands. He angled his head and aimed his gun across the kitchen, pretending to shoot down the people he was told to murder

"You ain't gotta worry about nothin', cuzzo. I got chu faded." Tristan swore, pretending to pull the trigger of his handgun.

"I had plenty of chances to waste you all, but I didn't take 'em with my tenda hearted ass. I let love get in the way of me avengin' my family. It took years but I finally pushed that shit aside." Tristan shut his eyelids briefly and shook his head. He then looked back up at Fear, "On some real shit, you and Eureka made it a lil' mo' easier for me to do it. You see, I could still see that she had love for you. Her mouth could tell whateva lies she willed it to, but her eyes…her eyes couldn't lie. It was from that, and lookin' at this fuckin' tattoo everyday that I finally got the balls to go through with it." He looked down at his fist. The L.O.E, Loyalty Over Everything, tattoo was on the side of his hand. It was the ink given to him when he was inducted into the fraternity by Eureka and Anton. The insignia was also worn by not only them, but Fear as well. Fear had given it to them over twenty years ago when he trained them up at the very mountain top he was trained. "Loyalty over everything; I started thinkin' about my loyalty and who it belonged to…rightfully. My loyalty belongs to my family…and Constance is my family."

"The Devil—The Devil Wears Timbs." Fear said, seeing that Tristan was in a pair of Timberland boots. He was still slumped and holding his stomach wound, both of his hands slicked with his blood.

"Indeed he does." Tristan smiled evilly and pointed his gun at Fear's forehead. His eyebrows sloped and his nose wrinkled. "This is for Constance."

Choot!

The shot went wild and struck one of the last standing portraits on the mantle, causing it to fall. The portrait was Tristan and Eureka's wedding picture. Tristan dropped his gun and his eyes bulged. He slowly turned around to see who had attacked him. When he did this, he revealed the butcher's knife sticking halfway out the back of his skull. Eureka, who'd stabbed him in the head with the butcher's knife, mad dogged him and spat the pills he'd given her into his face.

"When you get to hell, say hi to yo' punk-ass cousin for me," Eureka said as Tristan dropped to his knees and fell face-first to the carpet. Looking down at him, she hawked up some phlegm and spit on his dead body. "Fear," She looked up and seen the first man she'd ever loved slumped up against the fireplace. From the way he was looking she could tell he was on the verge of dying.

"Don't leave me! Please, don't leave me, baby." Eureka pleaded with Fear as tears cascaded down her cheeks. She picked up the cordless telephone and dialed 9-1-1, giving them a brief rundown. She then disconnected the call and tossed the telephone aside. Afterwards, she grabbed Fear by the collar of his suit and his right hand. With a grunt, she pulled him to his feet and threw his arm around her shoulders. Together, they made their way out of the mansion and down the front steps, trekking across the front lawn. Fear winced and limped along the way. When he coughed up blood, he knew he had a hole inside of his lung.

"Ahhhh, fuck!" Fear said, seeing he'd coughed up blood. Eureka looked at the blood he'd spat, and her eyes welled up with tears. She watched as he wiped his bloody lips with the back of his fist. "I can't—I can't make it any further. I'm—I'm sorry." He collapsed where he stood and brought her down with him.

Eureka crawled over to Fear, crying and dripping teardrops on his suit. She took his bloody hand into her hand and caressed it as she stared into his face. His face was sweaty and paling. His eyelids were narrowed into slits and his bottom lip trembled a little.

"No, no, no, don't say that," Eureka told him as she shook her head and more teardrops fell. "You're gonna be just fine, you're gonna be okay." She looked beyond the gates, which were opening, seeing and hearing the ambulance approaching hastily. "The ambulance is almost here, baby! Just hang on, you just gotta hang on!" Eureka looked down at Fear and his eyelids were nearly shut. His breathing was so shallow she couldn't tell if he was still alive or not. He looked dead. In fact, she had to check his pulse in his neck and listen to his heartbeat to make sure she hadn't lost him yet.

"I'm—I'm—I'm so tired, Eureka. I want to go to sleep." He said weakly.

"No, no, no," she sniffled. "Don't go to sleep. If you go to sleep then I'll never see you again. I already lost you twice already. I can't do it again; I can't lose the love of my life. Don't break my heart, baby. Don't break my heart again. Please, please, don't leave me. I'm begging you." She made the ugliest face as she sobbed. "Oh, my God, I love you. I love you so much."

A slight smile formed on Fear's lips and he reached up, rubbing the side of his hand against her cheek.

"I love you, too. I never stopped loving you, and I never will stop." Fear told her as he wiped the tears away from her dripping eyes, pulling her closer to him. Eureka laid her head against his chest and he wrapped his arm around her. He kissed the top of her head and laid his head back. He then shut his eyelids. By this time, the emergency sirens were getting closer and closer. Before either of them knew it, the ambulance was racing over the threshold of the estate and headed towards them.

Thirty-five years later

Fear and Eureka had Sunday dinner at their mansion which had become a family tradition. Their kids and their children showed up. They ate and talked among one another. As night ceased daylight, Fear's grandchildren begged him to tell them a story. He was reluctant at first, but he eventually gave in and told them a story.

"And that's the story of how I lost my hand…" Fear took off his prosthetic hand and held up his stump. He rotated his stump around the living room so that his children and grand children could see it. His children looked around at all of their kids wearing smirks on their faces as they stood beside their wives, girlfriends or husbands. Their children's eyes were as big as saucers and their mouths were hanging open. This was the first time they had been told the story of the fight their great uncle had with their grandfather.

"Can we touch it, Grandpa Al?" one of the boys asked. His hair was in cornrows and he looked a lot like Anton, surprisingly.

"Sure. Come on up here," Fear motioned the youngsta over with his stump. The boy hopped to his feet from where he was sitting Indian style with the rest of his siblings and cousins, listening to the story his grandfather had been telling them.

"Oh, oh, oh, oh!" a little girl stuck her hand up higher and higher in the air, excitedly. She was trying her best to be seen and called upon.

"Yes, Cee Cee?" Fear asked as he let his grandson he'd called up rub his stump.

"Can I come up and touch it, too?" Cee Cee asked.

Fear looked around the living room and saw that all of his grandchildren had their hands up in the air. He didn't even have to ask, he knew they all wanted to touch his stump. Until now they'd always seen him wearing his prosthetic hand over it. "How about all of you guys come up?" He motioned all of the children up with his stomp.

All of the kids hopped up to their feet and ran over to Fear. They stood around touching, rubbing and caressing his stump while asking him one hundred and one questions about it. He smiled and tried his best to answer them all, no matter how ridiculous they may have been.

"Here you go, baby." Eureka approached with a glass of water for Fear and his blood pressure pills.

"Thank you, baby." Fear kissed his wife. He then threw back the pills she'd given him and took the glass of water, washing down his medication. He passed the glass back to Eureka and grabbed her by the waist, sitting her down on his knee. She threw her arm over his shoulder and smiled, watching her excited grandchildren rub on his stump.

"Look at all of granny's babies." Eureka looked around at her grandchildren. She ruffled the hair of the one that looked the most like Anton and kissed the top of his head.

"Grandpa Al, tell us some more stories, please." One of the grandchildren asked. This little fella resembled Eureka and Anton's deceased father, Bootsy.

"Alright. One more, but that's it." Fear told him. "Y'all sit back down on the floor and I'll tell you about the time I rose to power in Brazil."

The children fled back to the carpet and sat down Indian style. Leaning forward, they propped their chin on top of their fists and listened intently to their grandfather's story. The entire living room was silent. They loved when their grandfather told them stories. He was the best story teller in the world to them, and no one could tell them different.

After Fear finished his epic story, his grandchildren were begging him for more but he thwarted their attention away with vanilla ice cream. As the children ate their delicious treat, the adults talked among themselves. Seeing the children getting sleepy, Fear and Eureka's kids had their offspring put on their coats and hugged and kissed their parents goodbye.

Fear closed the door behind the last of his guests to leave his home. He then turned around to Eureka smiling, holding her around her waist. She threw her arms around his shoulders and stared up into his eyes, lovingly. From the look in her eyes and the expression on her face you could tell she was still madly in love with him, like she'd always been.

"Who would have thought that two certified killaz from the streets would grow old together and live happily ever after?" Eureka said, bringing her lips closer to her man's lips.

"Yeah, who would have thought?" Fear kissed his lady, romantically. He then rested his forehead against her forehead, holding her gaze. They stood in silence, admiring and appreciating one another. "I love you."

"I love you even more." She swore to him.

They kissed again and he took her by her hand, leading her towards the staircase. "Come on, let's get ready for bed."

****

After showering and taking care of their hygiene, Eureka and Fear lay in bed. He lay behind her with his arms around her, his fingers interlocked with hers. The lights were out and the sounds of Heatwave's *Always & Forever* were serenading their time together. They didn't say a word to each other. They just lie in bed enjoying one another's presence.

Always and forever, each moment with you

Is just like a dream to me that somehow came true

And I know tomorrow will still be the same

'Cause we've got a life of love that won't ever change

And every day, love me in your own special way

Lying in the embrace of the one that they loved, eyelids shut and smiles etched across their lips, the married couple shared their last 'I love you'. Right after, they released their last breath and left this life for the blissfulness of the next.

After the elderly couple's lives expired, the song continued playing.

Melt all my heart away with a smile

Take time to tell me you really care

And we'll share tomorrow together

Ooh, baby, I'll always love you forever...

THE END

AVAILABLE NOW BY TRANAY ADAMS

The Devil Wears Timbs 1-7

Bury Me A G 1-5

These Scandalous Streets 1-3

A South Central Love Affair

Me And My Hittas 1-6

The Last Real Nigga Alive 1-3

God Bless the Trappers 1-3

A Gangsta's Empire 1-4

Fangeance

Fear My Gangsta 1-5

A Hood Nigga's Blues

The Realest Killaz 1-3

The Last of the OGs 1-3

The Streets Don't Love Nobody 1-2

The Dopeman's Bodyguard 1-2

King of the Trenches

ACKNOWLEDGEMENTS

Jasmine Devonish, Kim LeBlanc, Dorothea Creamer, Tamara Greene, Roneisha Cooper, Lashawn Green, Monique Williams, Christine Ms. Gemini, Sharon Bell, Jane Pannella, Viola King, Eliza Tellis, Standifur aka Fee, Michelle Harvey, Joan Brooks, Milly Ann, Jeannette Frazier, Delores Miles, Denise Moore, Erica Jackson, Quanisha Goss, Tracy Spicer, Genova Rhodes, Tanya Garry, Judy Richburg, Adaryl Fisher, Randy Coxton, Marius Clark, Alesha Kream, Nikki Hamilton, Larry L-Boogie Deadmon, Melissa Nicholson, Cyndy Twin, JS Queen, Diane Wilson, LaTasha Williams, Pamela Johnston Ward, Stephanie McL The Beast Reader, Michelle Chatman, Audreina Robinson, Desto ElGato.

THE DEVIL WEARS TIMBS VI

Let Me Holla At Y'all!

The Devil Wears Timbs is six books long. It has been a long run, but I have finally brought the series to an end. Now, originally I had ended the series in book three, but then I started getting asked about a part four from my readers. That's when I decided to keep the series going. I had renamed it The Realest Killaz because I didn't have the rights any longer. But once I got the rights back I went back to calling it TDWT

I wrote three more books to the series. On the fifth book I felt like I had ended the saga perfectly, but then I thought that Kingston had a story that needed to be told, and I also wanted to wrap up what was going on with Tristan, Eureka, Anton and Fear. I had written myself in a corner, so I was forced to write my black ass out of it!

It took me a while to knock out this book because I wasn't quite sure where to take the story. I had some ideas but they weren't finished. Once I started working on other novels, ideas for TDWT 6 began coming to mind, so I'd write in the document every once and a while. Things finally started coming together and making sense story wise, and before I knew it the story was done and here we are.

THE DEVIL WEARS TIMBS VI

Although I loved writing about these characters, after a while I became bored with them. I mean, you can't keep a story going and going just because your readers want you to. Don't get me wrong, I could keep a story going forever and ever, but not if I feel that there aren't any more stories to tell. You Griff me?

For those of you still wanting more of Fear, he has his own series out now. It's called, Fear My Gangsta. I plan on making it a four to five book series. That's it though. I hope you enjoy it.

Thanks goes to all of you beautiful, beautiful mothafuckaz for staying down with The Ink pen Pimp. I had a ball bringing you a series that you all know and love. It's been a pleasure!

I love y'all to life, 100!

www.ingramcontent.com/pod-product-compliance
Lightning Source LLC
LaVergne TN
LVHW021715060526
838200LV00050B/2668